# Venus Rocks

**phantorama** *n*. Very rare condition
which gives the ability to see ghosts.
Can be cool, but mostly just freaky…

# fiona dunbar

ORCHARD

ORCHARD BOOKS
338 Euston Road, London NW1 3BH
*Orchard Books Australia*
Level 17/207 Kent Street, Sydney, NSW 2000

First published in the UK in 2012 by Orchard Books

ISBN 978 1 40830 930 8

Text © Fiona Dunbar 2012

The right of Fiona Dunbar to be identified as the author of this work has been
asserted by her in accordance with the Copyright, Designs and Patents Act, 1988.

A CIP catalogue record for this book is available from the British Library.

3 5 7 9 10 8 6 4

Printed in Great Britain

Orchard Books is a division of Hachette Children's Books,
an Hachette UK company.

www.hachette.co.uk

**For Sara, Nick, Kate and Harry**

# Away with the Fairies

My next ghost appeared just when I least expected it.

It happens that way sometimes. When you have phantorama like I do, things can go quiet for a time. Not much ghost action. And then you can almost forget about it, and start to feel like everybody else. Like, I haven't written a *thing* in my ghost blog lately. Well, I call it a blog, but it's not on the internet or anything. God, no! I just have to write stuff, or I'd go crazy; it helps me make sense of things. But every now and then: blanksville. Until, *boom*, it happens. And I'm jerked back into all the weirdness again. Weirdness and mystery…

'And we-e-e-e-e're…*in* Cornwall!' announced Maro, as the Hippo whizzed past the 'Welcome to Cornwall' sign. The Hippo's our camper van: we kind of live in it now.

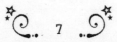

'Maro,' groaned Sam. 'We're not five years old any more, you know.'

'I know, *pethaki-mou*,' said Maro. 'But Cornwall's …different.'

It's true, Cornwall is different. You go through Somerset, Devon – even the northern bit of Cornwall – and it's all so *nice*, so well-behaved. So English. Then you get right down to the south-west, and it's this wild, end-of-the-world place. It's craggy, and rugged, and…all sorts of other words with double-g in them. And full of magic, too: stories that are kind of part of the land. Giants, pixies and all that.

Our Cornwall cousin, Ashley, was always big on that stuff. 'I wonder if she's grown out of it by now,' said Sam. 'I mean she is, what, fourteen by now, right?'

'Hey, I'm sixty-three, and *I'm* still into all that stuff,' said Maro.

'Yeah, but you don't *seriously* believe in giants and pixies,' said Flossie.

'Sure I do!' said Maro, but in that way she has that you know she's kidding.

'OK, well don't wind Ashley up, Sam,' I said, nudging him. 'I know what you're like.'

My brother, the sceptic; always so logical, and obsessed with facts: how I'd ever got him to believe in

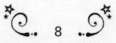

my phantorama was a mystery – oh, except for all the poltergeist activity he'd witnessed. There was no arguing with *that*.

Maro was all excited about seeing Aunty Phoebe – well, she would be, being her mum and everything. Phoebe reminds her of *our* mum – minus the phantorama. Yup, my mum's the one I got *that* bit of weirdness from. Thanks, Mum! She died when we were really small, so it's not like we especially missed her – plus we had Maro, who's the best parent we could ever have, even if she is technically a grandparent. But losing Mum meant that the only person I could've really got any solid advice from was gone (phantorama is incredibly rare. I mean, do *you* know anyone with it?).

I figured Maro must've told Phoebe about my phantorama by now – but actually she hadn't. 'I will one day of course, *pethaki-mou*,' she'd said, when I'd asked her about it. 'But not just yet. You're still getting used to it. The last thing you want is everyone asking you about it–'

'Worrying about me, wanting to know if I'm *OK* all the time…'

'Exactly!' said Maro.

I'd given a little sigh of relief. 'Good – thank you.' One less thing to deal with. But hey, I hadn't actually

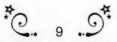

had any ghostly interactions for a while. Maybe things would be quiet in Cornwall, too…

Aunty Phoebe and Uncle Sean's place is all muddy wellies, animals, pet hairs, stuff and homework and Phoebe's pottery everywhere. Little dollops of bird poo here and there from the free-range pet cockatoo, Winston. It's a bit mad, but brilliant. I always loved visiting them, and this time we'd be staying longer than usual, because hey! We were free agents now. No school terms to fit around, what with Maro home-schooling us, no static home to get back to… Free as the wind!

Phoebe and Sean's is kind of a small house, but with loads of space to roam around outside. And by the time we'd arrived after our epic journey, we were *desperate* to do some roaming. So after a bit of chat over a slice of Phoebe's carrot and beetroot cake (*way* nicer than it sounds, even if it did look like a failed pottery experiment) we got to go outside.

Ashley, all bouncy with excitement, led us out into the fields at the back, where there were the large lichen-covered stones called the Giants' Quoits.

'I wanna go over to the Logan Stone!' said Flossie.

The Logan Stone had been a favourite spot ever since we could remember. We headed through scrubland

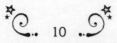

full of prickly yellow gorse bushes, and on to the coastal path, lined by dramatic rock-scapes. We could see the sea now, glistening in the last of the sunlight. And there it was: a large stone, flattish on top, rounded on the bottom, perched on top of a pile of rocks. It looked like it might roll off at any moment, but it was rock-solid, not budging a millimetre. According to legend, you *might* be able to move it – but only if you were 'completely pure of mind and deed'.

Ashley climbed up to it. 'So, Flossie: are you pure, or do you have the devil in you?'

'Oh, I'm definitely wicked,' said Flossie. 'I tried before.'

'Ah, but maybe the devil has left you now!' said Ashley. 'Go on, have a go!'

Flossie climbed up and gave the stone a little shove. Then she pushed a little harder. Finally, she stood up and leaned right into it with both hands. It didn't budge.

Ashley's uncombed strawberry blonde locks twisted in the wind as she laughed. 'Still wicked, then!'

'Yup,' said Flossie, jumping down. 'Guess so.'

We all had a go. You can't resist – even though you know it's impossible to move the stone, and the story is just one of those Cornish legends.

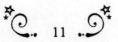

'Y'know, this is also a famous spot for sightings of spriggans,' said Ashley.

'What are spriggans?' asked Flossie.

'Oh, here we go,' muttered Sam.

I gave him a sharp nudge.

Ashley didn't hear. 'They're the spirits of the giants,' she said. 'And you have to be wary of them: they're tiny, but they retain their giant's strength and can be vicious – especially if you try to steal their treasure. They're often guarding treasure. Also, at times, they can grow to gigantic size.'

Flossie was fascinated. '*Really?*'

'No, not really, Floss,' said Sam, chuckling. 'It's just a folk tale.'

'What do you mean, "just" a folk tale?' said Ashley. 'Folk tales have real meaning, you know.'

'Of course they do,' I said, smoothing things over. I flashed Sam a look.

We headed back to the house, Ashley walking on ahead with Flossie, talking about spriggans.

'Yup – just as bonkers as ever,' said Sam.

I rolled my eyes. 'What did I say, Sam? Don't get on her case. So what if she believes in that stuff? I think it's kind of sweet, actually. I mean, deep down, don't we all kind of want to believe it? It's fun to picture it all.'

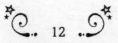

The low sun threw golden light onto the windows of the Hippo and Aunty Phoebe's little farmhouse. My lungs full of sea air, I sighed as I thought about the long Bank Holiday weekend stretching out before us. Summer was here. Rocky coves, sandy beaches, long, warm afternoons...I couldn't wait!

I woke up to the sound of the cock's crow. 'Woo! C'mon, wake up, Floss! Beach!'

'Yay!' Flossie leaped out of bed.

Then we looked out of the window, and there was nothing. Blank, white nothingness all around. Like we were in a cloud, or something.

'Oh.'

Cornish mist.

It can descend without warning, and last for days. Just sits there, blotting everything out. Sucking all the warmth and glow from the sun. So much for sun, sea and sand.

We went over to the house for breakfast. Aunty Phoebe and Uncle Sean were very apologetic, even though it wasn't their fault, of course. Ty was there, too: he's Ashley's big brother. Totally grown up, finished school and everything.

'Well, we'll have to think of a Plan B,' said Phoebe.

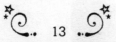

'Aaark!' cried Winston the cockatoo; he swooped across the room – I had to duck – and landed on Phoebe's head, as she was bringing a pile of toast to the table.

She just carried on, ignoring him. 'You could go out on the boat with Sean,' she suggested.

Uncle Sean's a marine biologist. Apparently his latest project involved cruising round the Cornish coast, counting fish. Some kind of global warming survey type thingy. How the hell you went about counting fish, I couldn't imagine…

'Mum, that's *boring*,' moaned Ashley.

'For you, maybe, Ashley, but what about your cousins?'

Winston balanced contentedly on Phoebe's head as she bustled back and forth, then took off and landed on Uncle Sean's head. 'Good idea!' he said, making it look as if having the bird on your head meant it was your turn to speak. He dolloped yogurt on his muesli. I couldn't help worrying he might get a dollop of something else if he wasn't careful, but he didn't seem concerned. 'It's misty, but there's no wind; the sea will be calm. I can think of one or two spots we could go to. You up for it, Ty?'

'Yeah,' said Ty, even though he didn't have a bird

on his head. 'I go down with this camera, you see, and the image is picked up on a monitor on the boat.'

'Oh, this is that diving training you've been doing!' said Maro.

'Well, no, the training's finished now,' said Ty, buttering a slice of toast. 'I'm fully qualified. So now I'm officially part of the research team.'

'So, hold on: we get to see what you see when you're down there?' asked Sam.

Ty nodded, his mouth full of toast. 'Mm-hmm.'

'Oh, cool...hey, can we dive too?'

'Not today, I'm afraid,' said Ty. 'But I'm sure we can get you on a course, if you're interested.'

'How long does it take?' I asked.

'Oh, you can learn in as little as a week, or even a couple of days,' said Ty.

Flossie shuddered. 'I don't want to dive, it would freak me out.'

'Ah well, you're a bit young anyway, Flossie,' said Sean.

'Are there any shipwrecks?' asked Sam.

Winston swooped over to Ty's shoulder. Ty nearly choked on his toast. 'Is Paris in France? This is Cornwall – of *course* there are shipwrecks!'

'Aark!' went Winston, which made us all laugh,

'cause not only did he make Ty look like your clichéd pirate, sitting there on his shoulder like that, but it sounded like he was agreeing with him.

So we went for it.

Having Sean actually working on a project here in Cornwall was unusual: half the time he was off in the Outer Hebrides or Florida or somewhere. On the outside the boat looked pretty much like any modern fishing boat, but then on the *inside*…somehow it actually seemed bigger, and crammed with monitors and stuff.

'Wow, it's like a Tardis!' said Flossie.

Sean laughed. 'Well, don't get your hopes up; I don't *think* we'll be doing any time-travelling.' He started up the boat, and slowly we made our way out of the harbour. Sam asked a gazillion questions, being Sam. 'What's this do? What's that for?' Sean and Ty patiently explained everything.

After we'd gone some way out, Ty went down with the camera, and we watched the monitor as the blank grey-green of the waters gave way to images of wafting seaweed, darting fish and barnacled rocks.

'So how many shipwrecks are there around here?' asked Sam, who'd obviously become fixated.

'Oh, hundreds are recorded off the coast of Cornwall,' said Sean. 'It's notoriously treacherous.

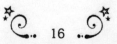

As well as the strong winds that can change direction without much warning, you've got the reefs down below; massive rock formations that you can't see. If the tide is low enough, they'll rip your hull apart. Even those rocks you *can* see can be pretty impossible to avoid in stormy conditions… Oh here, we are. See that?' he said, as a murky, rusty object appeared. 'That's the wreck of the *Auriole*, a cargo ship that went down in 1976; most of the crew were rescued, but not all, unfortunately.'

We watched as the camera glided around the barnacled wreck, shining its light on silvery shoals of fish as they weaved in and out of rusty panels. All of a sudden, *boo!* A face appeared in the foreground.

'Wah!' I cried, jerking back. 'Who's that?'

'Oh, nothing to do with us,' said Sean, as the diver waved at the camera, giving thumbs-up signs. 'You get divers around the wrecks. This is the prime season, good visibility; later on in the summer, the seaweed grows too thick. Those guys are just tourists, looking for souvenirs. You can still find interesting things among the wreckage – valuable things, even. Look at him…go away!' Sean shooed at the diver, although of course he couldn't see us. 'Thank you,' said Sean, when the camera finally moved away.

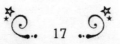

'So, you get, like, tour guides taking people to wrecks?' asked Sam.

'Mm-hmm,' said Sean. 'Or the more experienced divers can just get the locations from the internet.'

Sam frowned. 'How do you get directions for finding a shipwreck? I mean, it's not like they can say "turn left at the Post Office" or anything like that.'

Sean smiled. 'You get the coordinates,' he explained. 'You know: longitude and latitude? So you need global positioning equipment to get you to the location.'

'Oh, like SatNav in a car?' said Sam.

'Exactly.'

'Cool.'

The camera passed over the rusted hull of the boat again. Then another face appeared, and I jumped. This time I was horror-struck...because this one had no wetsuit, no breathing apparatus. Just a pale, bloated face, staring back at me with dead eyes.

# Spirits of the Drowned

'What's the matter?' said Uncle Sean.

'That...that...' The figure continued to drift upwards, and I saw more of him. He was puffy and pale, his shirt-tails waving around his swollen middle. The crown of his head was shiny and bald, edged by a thin curtain of drifting hair, and his pale eyes were like two gleaming soft-boiled eggs. A long fish – an eel, I guessed – swam in through his right ear and out of the left one. It was clear that he was very, very dead; it was also clear that no one else could see him.

'Er...that fish,' was all I managed to say.

'That's a juvenile conger eel,' said Uncle Sean. 'Very common around here. They grow up to three metres long.'

'Ah.' I said. My mouth was suddenly dry as paper. It was the unexpectedness of it that had given me

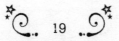

a fright; for some reason I just hadn't thought shipwrecks = dead people = underwater ghosts. Don't ask me why: it was pretty obvious, now I came to think about it. Poor old Mr 1976 was searching for someone else who'd been on board, I guessed; probably someone who'd been rescued. Well, he was either searching for some*one* or some*thing*. Which made me wonder: did the ghosts of drowned people ever come out onto land?

'Are you all right?' asked Sean. 'Are you getting seasick?'

'No, I'm fine,' I said. Sam and Flossie were looking at me, and had probably guessed what had happened. I avoided their gaze and turned back to the monitor.

More 1970s ghosts. Pretty soon I was just as used to the sight of them as I was to the ghosts I saw on land. Then the camera moved away from the wreckage, and it was back to the seaweed and the fish.

Until another figure came into view.

I thought it was a boy at first. Barefoot, and wearing cropped trousers that rippled around the figure's thighs. Baggy white shirt that billowed out under an ill-fitting jacket, and tendrils of fair hair that escaped from under a red headscarf. A boho beach bum type, I thought; the kind you see a lot of in Cornwall. Would probably be wearing a shark's tooth necklace, maybe have a piercing

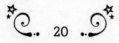

or two here and there. But as we got nearer, I could see that the limbs were too slender and hairless; it was a girl. Her face was pitted with little scars; you couldn't exactly call her pretty – more 'striking', I suppose. I never really understood what people meant by the word 'striking', but here was someone who seemed to fit that description exactly. She roamed around the sea bed, not seeming to care where she put her feet, as unaware of the flatfish and the crabs as they were of her. At one point she turned and gazed into the lens; her piercing blue eyes were red-rimmed and had dark circles underneath, like she hadn't slept in an age. Then she drifted away, disappearing into the misty waters.

*Damn!* I was used to these fleeting glimpses of interesting-looking ghosts. Occupational hazard. But…somehow this one was different. For some reason I couldn't get her out of my head. I guess partly because she was a girl, but a big part of it was just the fact that she was down there under the sea, yet no way was she anything to do with the *Auriole*. It wasn't just that she was further away; it was…something else about her. I couldn't say why, but she just didn't seem to fit. And she wasn't a 21st-century beach bum type, I'd realised when she'd got up close: those clothes seemed to belong to a much earlier time. What was her story? I wanted to

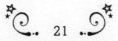

follow her – but I couldn't exactly ask Uncle Sean to do that.

'Uncle Sean?' I said, when I'd finally calmed down and got my head together.

'Yes?'

'I'd really like to learn scuba diving. Can I?'

'Diving! What a great idea, *fantastika*!' said Maro, clapping her hands. Since she home-schooled us, she thought a short course in scuba diving would be a brilliant boost to our education. And about a gazillion times better than hour upon hour of dreary maths, if you ask me. Plus more useful. Well, possibly. Definitely if you have a mysterious underwater ghost to investigate.

Only problem was, we were too late for that weekend's course. The soonest we'd be able to start was Tuesday. I nearly went off the idea when Sean told us the first two days were just sitting at the desk learning the theory stuff – but not quite. Meanwhile if the weather was going to go on being lousy, we'd have to figure out what the hell to do with ourselves for the next couple of days.

Groan.

And yes, the lousy weather did drag on. By lunchtime the mist was still as thick as ever, and now it was combined with a fine drizzle – 'mizzle', as they call it. We

hung out at the house all afternoon. Aunty Phoebe's house was so in the middle of nowhere, they didn't even have broadband...how they managed without the internet, I couldn't imagine, but they didn't seem to care. So we mucked about in Phoebe's pottery studio, played computer games, ducked to avoid the swooping cockatoo, and tripped over cats (there were three in all). By the evening we were actually playing charades, that's how desperate things got.

'I do hope the weather improves by Monday,' said Phoebe.

'Oh, it will, Phoebe, it will,' said Maro.

'Why, what's on Monday?' I said.

'It's the May Day festival,' said Phoebe. 'Ashley's taking part in it – aren't you, Ashley.'

'Oh? What are you doing?' I asked her.

'Singing,' she said. 'Come upstairs, I'll show you,' she added, all eager-beaver. I followed her up.

She closed the door behind her and beamed at me, brimming with excitement. 'Kitty. Have you got a boyfriend?'

I blinked at her. 'Me? Oh, no. I mean, I'm not even in school any more, so–'

'I have!' said Ashley, obviously just *dying* to tell me about him.

'Yeah?'

She nodded frantically. 'Mm-hmm! He's called Oliver, and I swear he's my soulmate. He's in the choir, same as me; we'll be singing together in the festival!'

'Oh. That's nice.' *Oliver*, I thought. Sings in the choir. Probably wears turtlenecks. Bet his mum cuts his hair. 'I guess I'll meet him soon,' I said.

'Well, he's quite shy,' said Ashley. 'Doesn't say much. But he's lovely.' Suddenly she snatched up the guitar that was propped against the wall next to the bed. 'Hey, I wrote a song! It's kind of for him, but he doesn't know it yet. You want to hear it?' Then she launched straight into it anyway.

I'm not used to having people burst into song at me, so I didn't know where to look. I mean, what do you *do* in that situation: just sit there, grinning at them? Noooo! So I just kind of mooched about, picking up bits of dusty pottery and jewellery and stuff while she warbled away. The lyrics were really cheesy but at least her singing wasn't bad, or I'd have just died of embarrassment.

The rest of the evening was taken up with eating. And eating. Well, there wasn't much else to do. *Really* hoped tomorrow would be better…

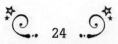

I've just had the weirdest dream. I was out at some random Cornwall beach, all by myself. It was cold and rainy, but then the clouds disappeared, the sun came out, and it became blisteringly hot (ha! I wish). I went out on the rocks, stripped down to my swimsuit and dived into the water. In the dream I could breathe underwater – and I could see everything, just like in those documentaries in tropical waters. Then a girl, fully clothed, popped up from behind a rock…it was the ghost with the red headscarf. She stared her red-rimmed stare and beckoned to me. I swam over – but then she turned, and as the rest of her appeared from behind the rock, I saw that she had a tail. A mermaid! She swam away, but I couldn't keep up, so I thought, I know what, I'll grow a fish's tail, too. Then I'll be able to keep up with her…

The dream ended – and now I can't get it out of my head. I think I can officially say (o-fish-ally??! Har har) that I'm obsessed. I NEED to find out more about her. Who is she? What's her story? I have to find out somehow. Although clearly, growing a fishtail ISN'T an option…

# Ghost Ship

Sunday: *still* misty. I really wanted to go out on the boat again, but Uncle Sean was having a day off. And we still had another two whole days to wait before we could start the diving lessons.

On and on with the mizzle; occasional bouts of heavy rain lashing away at the windowpane. It was starting to do our heads in. The windows steamed up. We ate Sean's home-made veggie soup; it was very gloopy. Gloopy soup. Gloopy, soupy air all around, inside and out. Noise and stuff and cats and bird. *Aark!* went Winston, describing exactly how I felt.

By 3 pm I really thought I was going crazy. So when Ashley asked if I wanted to go with her to her choir rehearsal, well, anyone would think she'd just presented me with a VIP ticket to the hottest West End show. 'Yeah!' I practically shrieked. 'That'll be great!'

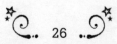

Anything to get out of the house – even if it was still mizzly out there. Plus, I'd get a look at this Oliver, the love of her life.

The village hall smelled of tea and stale cake and mothballs.

Everyone stared at me; I guess I still looked kind of London-y in my messy mismatched layers-scarves-bangles thing, whereas most of them were nice sensible choir kids in jeans and jumpers. The only ones who didn't stare were a small group at the far side of the room; some girls (the choir was nearly all girls) and a boy.

'There he is!' whispered Ashley. She took me by the arm and rushed me over. 'Hello, Oliver!' she gushed. 'Thisis-my-cuzzin-Kitty-they're-staying-withus.'

'Oh, hi…'

I gave a quick little wave and a smile.

He *so* wasn't what I expected. That definitely wasn't a mum-haircut, for starters; he had the sort of careless windswept look you only got from 45 minutes in front of the mirror with the hair gel and straighteners. No turtleneck; just a long-sleeved shirt with a Led Zeppelin T-shirt over it. And he was fit, I can't lie. Not my type especially, but fit.

'Sorry 'bout the weather,' he said. Ashley laughed

too loudly, as if it was some sort of hilarious joke; he gave her a quizzical look.

'It's s'posed to be better tomorrow,' said one of the girls.

*That's what they said yesterday*, I thought. 'Cool,' I said, nodding.

Then, thank god, the choir instructor clapped her hands together, and rounded them up for the rehearsal. Ashley attached herself to Oliver's side like a limpet; he didn't seem to care especially one way or the other, just sort of resigned himself to it. But nothing about the way they were together suggested to me 'soulmates': you could tell from the lack of eye contact. He barely looked at her at all. Poor Ashley – she was obviously a bit deluded.

I hung around politely for a couple of numbers, then slunk out. Hell, I wasn't going to stick around and get even more bored out of my brains than I already was! Ashley wouldn't mind; as long as I was back in an hour's time, it didn't matter what I did.

At least the rain had eased off. Pelporth was all wet stone and glistening slate. Smoke was drifting out of chimneys – ha! In *May*. That's how cold it was. I made my way down the steep cobbled hill towards the harbour. Brightly painted storefronts displayed windchimes and

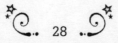

polished stones; a few grim-faced tourists in shorts, sandals and anoraks drifted from the pasty shop to the sweet shop to the cream teas place. Not much else to do. Pasty, fudge, clotted cream scones...then start all over again.

Seagulls screeched overhead. Somehow, no matter how many scavenging seagulls we used to get in London, I always got a thrill at the sound of the seaside ones. So few other noises to compete with them around here; just the crashing of the waves, the occasional outboard engine...

I twisted my way through the medieval cobbled streets, dodging ghosts of short people who emerged from tiny dollhouse doorways. They loomed out at me from the mist; they appeared around the corners of hidden alleys. One leaned on a windowsill overhead, smoking a pipe; another watered petunias outside the Mermaid Inn; she turned and smiled at me. 'Good morning!' Well, how would she know if it was morning or afternoon?

Down at the harbour, the tide was all the way out. Boats sat tilted on the soggy sand, while gulls and sandpipers poked around. A little boy crouched and picked up fistfuls of gloopy sand, watched by his mum. Up on the harbour wall was a grungy-looking gang of

older teens, mucking about. Drinking from cans, smoking, and playing some sort of game that involved a lot of shoving, jeering, laughing and swearing. And teetering about so much I thought someone was going to fall off the harbour wall. You could tell from their accents that they were locals.

They came nearer; the little boy's mum quickly cleaned up his hands and led him away. One of the teenagers accidentally lost her shoe; another picked it up and threw it, and it landed near my feet. The girl yelled at him jokily, and ran over to collect it. Her hair was unusual: sandy-coloured, pink-tinged dreadlocks that flapped heavily as she ran. I picked up the worn-out canvas shoe and handed it to her. 'Thanks,' she muttered, not looking at me. She hopped about on one foot as she put it back on, then went on yelling at her friend. I watched her as she went back to them, curious; she didn't seem old enough to be hanging out with them.

Then I looked away, not wanting to stare. Glancing towards the headland, I spotted a figure with a red headscarf, climbing the steep wooden staircase that led away from the harbour. It was too misty to make the figure out clearly but, crazy though this sounds, I got it into my head that it might be my underwater ghost.

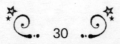

Well, it *might*. After all, how often did you come across someone in a red headscarf?

The figure was nearing the top of the headland; I hurriedly climbed the steps to try and catch up. I lost sight of her, but kept going till I got to the top. Then I caught a glimpse of her again, crossing the headland to Bosreath Cove, where we'd been yesterday.

It was seriously windy up there, but I noticed the mist seemed to be clearing. At last! I could just about make out the horizon now. I looked down into the bay, but it was deserted. Then, once again, a blob of red, far below. Was that her?

She was all the way down on the pebbly, seaweedy beach. How did she get there? I scrambled down as far I could, but after that it was all gorse bushes, and a sheer drop. Had she somehow got there from the other side of the bay? It was still too misty to see across to the other side.

Oh, if only I could speak to her! I called out, 'Hallooo!' but it was no good; the wind completely swallowed up my voice. I gazed around helplessly; nope, there really was no way down from here.

On she walked across the beach, then disappeared into a cave.

I sat there for…I don't know how long. Waiting for

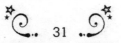

her to come out. I really wanted to know more about her, because she'd obviously died very young; what was her story? Drowned, most probably – but how? Capsized boat, sunken ship? Suicide? Murder? And how long ago?

I was so busy thinking and waiting, I lost track of the time: oops! Five past four. And no signal on my phone. I scrambled back up to the headland, and down into Pelporth Bay. Then my phone sprang back to life with a text message from Ashley; they were running over time. I called her back.

'You want to just meet up back at the house?' she suggested. 'Might be easier; you know the way, right?'

'Yeah…OK. See you there.'

I thought about sneaking another quick visit to Bosreath Cove, but until I could figure out a route right down to the beach, there didn't seem much point. You probably had to go all the way round to the other side, but there was no way of telling. Maybe Ashley would know.

I headed back.

Over on the other side of Pelporth Bay, there was another steep climb up some rocky steps, leading to the Logan Stone. From there it was down the hill through the scrubland. Only…when I got to the end of the gorse bushes, I found myself in a cow-field, instead of where

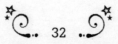

the Giants' Quoits were. Damn! I must've taken the wrong path through the scrub. I turned back and trudged back up the hill, to the Logan Stone; from there, I'd surely be able to figure it out.

When I got to the Logan Stone, I tried calling Ashley, just to check the route, but still there was no signal. Turning this way and that, trying to connect, I noticed a ship sailing into Pelporth Harbour. The mist had cleared enough for me to make out the harbour – just – though everything was kind of faint and flat, like it was behind a sheet of tracing paper. But the ship was impressive all the same. Three tall masts and billowing sails; *majestic* was the word that sprang to mind. Yes, majestic – and probably very old. *Must be something to do with the festival*, I thought. Old ships like that surely didn't get used on a regular basis.

Then something weird happened.

The ship kept going, right into the harbour. But the tide was still out, I was sure of it – it wasn't possible to sail that far! And yet there it was, gliding onward, in full sail. That was the other strange thing: I didn't know much about sailing, but common sense said you wouldn't want the wind pelting into full sails if you were coming into dock! You'd need to slow right down.

I needed to get a better look. Not taking my eyes off

the ship for a second, I made my way back towards the stone steps that led down into the village. Now the ship was right on the slipway and still going, about to crash into the Mermaid Inn. Yet as far as I could see, no one was trying to do anything about it. In fact, nobody seemed to notice. And then, as I got nearer, the ship just merged with the buildings, turning transparent. Finally, it disappeared altogether.

I came to a halt, still staring at the spot where it had been. I must have veered off the steps, because the next thing I knew, there was the screech of a gull, and I snapped out of my trance. And in front of me was–

Nothing.

Thin air.

The white water crashing and swirling among the rocks below.

I was perched right on the edge of a rocky outcrop, about to step off.

# Deadly Vision

'What happened to you?' said Ashley. She was sitting in the den with Sam and Floss.

'Oh, sorry I'm late,' I said, trying to sound all nonchalant. 'I took a wrong turn, and–'

'No, no, I don't mean that,' she said, standing up. 'I mean…look at you, you're white as a sheet. What's up?'

'Nothing's up!' I insisted. 'I'm fine.'

'You do look kind of pale,' said Flossie.

I couldn't go into it…I just couldn't. Not in front of Ashley, anyway. 'I am? Well, I got a bit lost…I guess I'm tired. I probably just need cake.'

'No, you're hiding something,' said Ashley, coming towards me. 'You keep looking away.'

Damn. Was I really? And I thought I was being pretty convincing. 'That's just 'cause I'm looking out for

Winston,' I said. 'I don't want him swooping up and flapping in my face.'

'Winston doesn't *do* that,' said Ashley. 'And you are *so* hiding something. You were doing it when we were on Dad's boat, too. Wasn't she, Sam?'

Sam looked uncomfortable. 'Well…'

Ashley took hold of me by the shoulders. 'Come on, Kitty. If it's secret we won't tell, promise.' She pushed the door shut. 'I shared something private with you,' she added, 'fair's fair.'

*But this is a much bigger deal than that!* I felt like saying. Telling her what I'd seen would probably involve giving everything away about my phantorama. On the other hand…I needed some help in making sense of what had just happened.

'OK, OK!' I said at last. 'I saw this weird ship. Down in Pelporth Bay. An old-fashioned sailing ship…and the weirdest thing of all is, it—'

Ashley gasped, silencing me. 'It sailed right into the town,' she said, wide-eyed.

I blinked at her. 'Y-yeah. How did you know?'

Ashley looked white. 'Oh Kitty, thank god you're still alive!'

'What? Why?'

'You've seen the *Venus*. That's a terrible omen!'

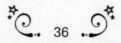

'Oh, give me strength!' said Sam, rolling his eyes.

Ashley ignored him. 'Kitty, this is serious. The *Venus* disappeared off the coast in 1728. They've never found the wreck, but there've been loads sightings of it over the years, exactly the same as you've just had. And everyone who saw it had something terrible happen to them soon afterwards.'

'No!' cried Flossie. 'That can't be true!'

'Don't worry, Floss, it's just some silly superstition,' said Sam.

'1982,' said Ashley. 'Harriet Jenkins: fell to her death from the cliffs. 1957, Norman Cavendish: drove his car off the headland. 1929, David Bunhill—'

'All right, enough!' I said. I thought of how I'd ended up heading for the rocky outcrop, just as if, as if… No. Had the sighting of that ship really made me want to throw myself off? I felt my flesh creep.

Sam was really annoyed now. 'You have no proof whatsoever that those people's deaths had anything to do with sightings of some…what is it, a ghost ship?' he said. 'Don't take any notice, Kit.'

'How many more do you need to hear about before you're convinced?' asked Ashley. '1901, Evelyn—'

'Shut *up*,' said Sam.

My insides were churning, but I sure as hell wasn't

going to let on about that. I tried to laugh the whole thing off instead. 'Oh, stop it, you two! Anyway, looks like I got off lightly, doesn't it? So nothing to worry about.' I thought some more. 'I mean, not that it's OK to tell anyone else...you know, in case *they* take it seriously. You'll stick to your promise and keep quiet, right, Ashley?'

'But that was before I–'

'No: nobody. You understand? Look, I'm not at risk now, so–'

'You don't know that!' said Ashley. 'Sometimes there are second or third sightings...the power grows stronger. This is dangerous!'

'Fine, then you guys can look after me, OK? No adults. Not that I think they'd believe it, but just in case they do. I don't fancy being a prisoner the whole time I'm here. Besides...' I trailed off, not knowing whether to tell her the whole story or not.

'What?' said Ashley.

'All right, look, there's something else you should know, Ashley. I see ghosts all the time. It's something called phantorama, and it's extremely rare. To be honest, I've probably already seen...oh, like, *dozens* of ghostly apparitions that have been bad omens. And nothing bad has happened to me yet.'

Ashley's jaw hung open. 'Really? What, all your life?'

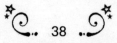

'No, just for the last two…years,' I lied. If Ashley thought I'd had this thing for two years instead of just two months, it'd be easier to convince her that I'd seen it all, and this was no big deal. Fortunately, Flossie didn't contradict me; I knew Sam wouldn't. 'So I really don't think it's the same as when other people see these things – people without phantorama. I reckon I'm probably immune – like someone who's been vaccinated, you know?'

'She's right,' said Sam quickly, before Ashley could say anything. 'There's your answer, Ashley. Even if you believe the stories–'

'Facts,' interrupted Ashley. 'And anyway, whether you believe or not makes no difference – you can still be affected.'

'Well, in this case, even if you believe the *stories*,' repeated Sam, 'it's nothing to worry about.'

---

**GHOST BLOG**
**SUNDAY 1 MAY**

OK, I'll admit it: I'm feeling just a little bit freaked out here. No: not a little bit: a LOT. Because if I'm honest about this, deep down I believe Ashley's story. I know

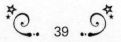

how close I came to walking straight off the edge of the rocks there. What if it happened again? What if, despite all their efforts, Ashley or whoever was with me couldn't stop me from going over the edge?

FACT: I saw the VENUS.

FACT: Other people have died after seeing it.

FACT: I've only had my phantorama for two months, and to my knowledge this is the first time I've ever seen anything that's supposed to signal my own doom.

OK, now I'm going to put on my Sam head, and question all of this.

1. There's no proof it was the Venus I saw. Could be another ship. With my phantorama, I might see lots of ghost ships. (Question: how can something man-made have a ghost? Hmm…)

2. There's no proof that those stories about the other people who died are true or not. Plus, accidents happen.

3. Ashley is crazy, and not to be believed about anything. And her beliefs are NOT harmless: they are harmful, if she convinces people that their lives are in danger.

Ghost ship. A GHOST of a SHIP. OK, still with my Sam head on: this is nonsense. You can't have a spirit of an inanimate object. You wouldn't have a ghost of

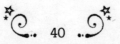

a chair, would you? But I SAW it. How do you explain that?

And how come the wreck of the Venus has never been found? FIND OUT MORE.

Problem: No point asking Uncle Sean. Ashley says she's asked him about the Venus before, and he didn't know much.

Is there someone else I can ask? Or get Ashley to?

OK, now NOT with my Sam head on:

Supposing it WAS the Venus I saw, and this whole bad omen business is true…then the SAME THING WILL HAPPEN TO OTHER PEOPLE in the future. And maybe, just MAYBE I can stop that from happening.

SO:

1. Find out more about the other people who saw it. Ashley knew their names off by heart. There would be a record of their deaths.

2. What did they have in common? Anything? Could THEY have had phantorama?

---

# Jane Doe

I woke up to a Hippo flooded with sunlight.

'Ya-hay!' cried Flossie, flinging open the curtains. 'The mist has gone, the mist has gone!'

I leaped out of bed and gazed at the dewy orchard, shimmering in the morning sun. 'Thank god for that! Oh wow…looks like a lovely day.'

'Yay!'

'Perfect!' said Maro. 'I said the mist would clear for the festival – and it has! Phoebe will be pleased.'

The sunshine lifted my mood for a little while – until I started thinking about the *Venus* again. It was like I'd been hit by a mini one-person-sized earthquake – and I was still getting the aftershocks. Every time I thought about something else, suddenly a tremor would run through me, and I'd be reliving those moments all over again. But finding out more wasn't going to be easy

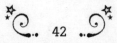

today; it was a bank holiday, plus pretty much the whole day was going to be taken up by the festival. Argh. Maybe the festival would take my mind off things. Ha! Who am I kidding?

When it was time to go, Ashley roped me into walking into the village with her, separate from the others. Unsurprisingly, she couldn't wait to bombard me with questions about my phantorama.

I don't like to tell people about that, and this is one reason: all the questions. 'What's it like, seeing ghosts all the time?' etc, etc. How do you answer that? 'Well, it's like seeing ghosts all the time.' It's a bit exhausting. If I could just once in my life talk to someone else who *knows* what it's like…oh yes! That would be so good…

About halfway down the rocky steps that led into the village, I suddenly had an idea. There *was* someone I could ask about the *Venus*…

'What's the creepiest ghost you've ever come across?' asked Ashley.

'Erm…' I speeded up a bit. The house was just about here, if I remembered right… Ah! Here it was. 'Oh, look, it's Bill's place,' I said.

Bill. *He* was the person I needed to talk to. Don't know why I didn't think of it before. He was a retired fisherman who lived in a tiny stone cottage set into the

hillside. Everyone knew Bill; I only visited once a year and even *I* knew Bill. I wouldn't be surprised if he was listed as an attraction in the Pelporth tourist guide. If you imagine someone running a giant comb through the village and the harbour, and dumping everything it collected there, you'll have some idea of what Bill's terrace was like. Old ropes and fishing nets draped everywhere, with bright red buoys dangling about. Assorted rocks and stones and pieces of rotting furniture. And lobster pots, and pieces of driftwood, and all manner of what most people would consider rubbish, fixed up as only Bill knew how, and made pretty with pot plants. A garden gnome supported a wooden box marked:

### DoNatiOns WeLcoMe!

Because Bill's terrace was a work of Art, and he wanted you to show your appreciation. Times were hard: when Bill found he wasn't making enough money at fishing he'd jacked it in. Now he just did odd jobs for people – badly. He wasn't much in demand.

'Can we just speed up a little?' said Ashley. 'I don't really want to get–'

'Oh, hello, Bill!' I called out, suddenly spotting him as he pottered around in the side passage by the cottage.

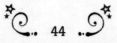

Bill looked up and waved at us, grinning his stumpy-toothed grin. 'Ah, halloo there!'

'Hello, Bill,' Ashley said. 'Erm…you remember my cousin Kitty, right?'

'Ah yes, yes, from London, right? Hallo!' Bill shook my hand; his own was rough as sandpaper. 'My, ent you grown! Sorry 'bout the weather, an' all…still, better now, eh? Bin here long, 'ave you?'

'Just since Friday,' I said. 'We went out on Ashley's dad's boat on Saturday, didn't we, Ashley?'

'Yeah.'

'Yes, we were looking at shipwrecks…well, *a* shipwreck.'

'What one'd that be, then?' asked Bill. 'The *Henrietta*? The *Auriole*? I knows all of 'em.'

'I don't remember,' I said. 'It was a 1970s one…'

'The *Auriole*,' said Bill. 'I remember that 'un. Shouldn't never of come so near, not, wi' that south-easterly blowin'.'

Just as I'd hoped: Bill knew about this stuff. 'Uncle Sean says there's loads of shipwrecks around here,' I said. 'It's pretty dangerous, right? I guess you'd know a lot about all that?'

'What I don't know 'bout navigatin' these here waters ain't worth knowin',' said Bill. 'Thirty-five year

a fisherman, I were; got salt water runnin' through my veins. You learns the seascape like the back o' your hand; the good routes, the bad ones…the outright no-go zones. There's a few of *them*, I tell yer. Spots you wouldn't go near for love nor money.'

I didn't know Bill was such a mine of information. 'What do you know about the *Venus*?' I asked.

Bill's face turned grave. 'The *Venus*? Ah yes…1728, if I remember rightly. Terrible business. They never did find the wreck of that one, I 'spect you know.'

'Why do you think that is, Bill?' I asked.

'Ah, it happens. You know the story o' Jane Doe?'

'No.'

'Well, they call 'er that, but it ent her real name,' said Bill. 'No one ever knew her real name. Strange story. Rumoured to be a survivor from the *Venus*; the only one ever found – though she were never identified. Young thing, she were, an' dressed like a cabin boy…'

My ears pricked up. Girl! Dressed as a cabin boy! Could it be…?

'She were washed up on shore three days later,' said Bill.

'How did they know she had anything to do with the *Venus*, then, and wasn't just some random drowned person?' asked Ashley.

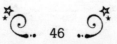

'Well, her right hand were shut tight as a clam, see?' said Bill. He held up his clutched fist. 'But they got it open. And inside they found a medal belonging to one Jed Lannion – had 'is name inscribed on it an' everything. Well, Jed Lannion were a sailor went down with the *Venus.*'

Ashley and I looked at each other.

'Here, you ent *seen* the *Venus*, either of you, I hope?'

We shook our heads vigorously. 'No...no.'

'Good,' said Bill. 'Saints preserve us, hope you never do.' He turned to me gravely. 'There's those as have seen it–' he began.

'I told Kitty all about what happened to them,' said Ashley.

'Ah, well, then, you know,' said Bill. 'Terrible business...'

I felt a shudder run through me. Having Bill confirm Ashley's story made it feel all too real. It made me nauseous...

I didn't dare ask Bill any more about the *Venus*, but I did want to know about that drowned girl. 'This Jane Doe,' I said. 'You wouldn't happen to know what she looked like, would you?'

'Jane Doe? Not much account o' that. Why d'you ask?'

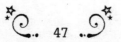

I gave him what had become my usual answer in these cases. 'I'm doing a project,' I explained. 'On shipwrecks in the area. Would be good to have pictures.'

Bill grimaced. 'Well, it's not like they had photographs back in them days. The body were probably decomposing...'

'Oh no, no, that's not what I meant!' I said. 'I mean, like, maybe a drawing – you know, of her *alive*...oh, but they didn't know who she was, so I guess there wouldn't be any...never mind.'

'Plus, back in those days only important people got their portrait done,' said Ashley.

'Ah, but you can do your own drawing for your project!' said Bill brightly. 'Use your imagination!'

I smiled weakly.

'Hey, you should come an' have tea some day with me an' our Megan,' Bill said to Ashley. 'Bin a while!'

Ashley gave him a rather forced smile and nodded. 'Yeah, lovely! Well, I'd better go, Bill. I'm singing in the festival.'

'Sure, sure, you go on,' said Bill. 'Say hello to Megan if you see 'er.'

'Bye!'

We waved to him and carried on down the hill.

'Awkward!' said Ashley.

'I could tell. What's up? Who's Megan?'

'She's his daughter,' said Ashley. 'We were at primary school together. But she's really changed; I don't have anything to do with her now. She doesn't go to school, or anything!'

'Erm, neither do I,' I said.

'No, no; you know what I mean!' said Ashley. 'She hangs out with this gang, gets into trouble all the time…'

'Oh hang on; she doesn't have pinkish dreadlocks by any chance, does she?'

'Oh, you've seen her already, have you?' said Ashley. 'Might've known; they're like a permanent fixture in the village, just bumming around, being useless.'

I told her about her losing her shoe. 'So what, she's only fourteen?'

'Fifteen,' said Ashley. 'But yeah, kind of young for that sort of thing. The others are like, seventeen, eighteen…I s'pose she thinks she's being all grown-up, hanging around with them, when really she's being a total loser.'

'What a shame…poor Bill.'

'Bill's *hopeless*,' said Ashley. 'He hasn't got a clue; he believes what he wants to believe about Megan, and ignores all the rest. So now you know why I wanted to avoid him. He's always trying to involve me, thinks I'm

a good influence or something. But I don't *want* to be involved!'

'But Ashley–'

'Anyway, come on,' said Ashley, grabbing me by the wrist. 'I'm going to be late for my performance if we don't hurry up.'

# The Man in the Leather Coat

The village was completely bustling with activity: you know, the usual village fair stuff. Punch & Judy for the teeny-tinies down on the quayside; bungee-jumping for the older kids. Somebody was striding around on stilts. Lots of stalls selling jam and cheese and Cornish pasties. We went up through the narrow village streets, and again I saw my pipe-smoking ghost and the flower-watering one; what was their unfinished business, I wondered? The sound of an accordion wafted our way, and I thought, ah yes, the Morris Men. Then we came out into the square by the village hall, and yup, there they were with their hats and their white trousers and their bells and their sticks. Bonkers.

We caught up with the others, and I saw the grungy gang cruising through the crowd. 'There they are again,' I said to Ashley. 'That's Megan's lot, right?'

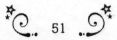

Ashley grimaced. 'Yeah, that's them…though minus Megan, for some reason.'

'Oh yeah…'

'Who's Megan?' asked Sam.

'She's the daughter of that guy Bill – you know, the one with the cottage with all the stuff outside? Ashley went to school with her, but now all she does is hang out with that lot.'

'All right, never mind them,' said Ashley. 'Come on, I'm on soon.'

We made our way through the crowd towards the little stage in front of the stream. The Morris Men finished; everyone clapped, and they jangled sweatily off. Maro, Phoebe and Sean beamed proudly as Ashley and the other choir members gathered together on the stage. Ashley shimmied her way over to Oliver and glued herself to his side, niftily using her bum to nudge another girl into the row behind them as she did so. The girl teetered slightly, and regained her balance. Oliver coughed and inspected his shoes.

Honestly. Did Ashley really have no idea? Talk about denial, I thought.

They started their performance. I stuck around for a couple of numbers just to be polite, then whispered to Sam, 'Back in a bit,' and sloped off.

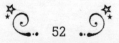

All I could think of was my ghost.

Well, actually, all I could think of was the *Venus*. But that's exactly why I was now even more obsessed with this Jane Doe, or whatever her name was. Because even though by now I'd got pretty good at connecting with spirits, there wasn't any way that was going to happen with the *Venus*, as it was just a ship. You can't talk to a ship! And even if there were human spirits inside it, I'd be too terrified to try to communicate with them because they were probably the malicious ones trying to lure me off a cliff or whatever. And I sort of wanted to go on living.

So maybe dealing with someone supposedly connected to the ship was the next best thing. No, it didn't really make much sense to me either – but what else could I do? I had to do whatever I could, just in case Ashley and Bill weren't both complete fruitcakes, and the story actually turned out to be true.

*OK: first thing*, I thought, as I weaved through the crowded village to the harbour, *find out if the ghost with the red headscarf really is Jane Doe. Let's not get ahead of ourselves here; she might not be.*

Actually, first thing would just be to find her again. Looking for her underwater wasn't an option; even though I'd be doing that diving course, Uncle Sean had

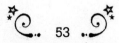

said it'd be ages before I'd be expert enough to go down deep. But if it was her I'd seen wandering up to the headland and down in Bosreath Cove, then that meant she did sometimes appear on land. It was worth trying to summon her.

Trouble was, I didn't even know her name. And I hadn't connected with her yet; she didn't know me. So far I'd figured out that phantorama can be a two-way thing; sometimes ghosts will home in on me, if they sense a connection. But so far with this one, it had only been one-way: I'd seen her, but *she* hadn't seen *me*. What link was there between me and Jane Doe? None. Well, apart from the ship thing – maybe. *If* she was Jane Doe…oh, I was going round in circles!

The tide was all the way in now, and the waves were crashing against the black rocks of the headland. I began the steep, windy climb to the top. There was a sharp bend in the flagstone steps about three-quarters of the way up; from this point there was a rough path that went in the other direction, towards the tip of the first rocky outcrop. As I was going round this bend, I heard a piercing cry – almost like a seagull's, but not quite. I turned around; down below, I saw a couple of figures near the end of the path; a girl and a man.

They were quite some way off, but I could tell

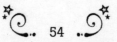

straight away that the girl was Megan; those pink-tinged dreadlocks were unmistakeable.

I quickly dipped under the iron handrail that lined the main path, and found some rocks to crouch behind; from there I had a pretty good view of them. Even though the buffeting winds carried off all but the loudest noise at this distance, I could tell this was not a friendly discussion. Megan was waving her arms quite a bit, like she was protesting, while the man – considerably taller than her – loomed over her, looking vaguely threatening. He was in his mid-twenties, I guessed, and definitely not grungy like Megan and her mates; his dark hair was much shorter and neater, and he wore a long black leather coat and jeans.

Who *was* this guy? What the hell was Megan doing out here with him? Whatever the reason, it didn't look like good news. I found myself clutching my phone in my pocket, ready to make an emergency call – if there was any signal, which there probably wasn't.

The argument dragged on; now it looked as if Megan was crying. OK, this was making me seriously uncomfortable. I checked my phone: nope, no signal. Well, I wasn't going to let this continue; she might get hurt. I scrambled back under the railings to the rocky pathway, then stood up so they'd know they weren't

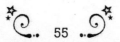

alone. Still they didn't see me, so I tried jumping about a bit…at last, the man seemed to notice me. I turned and carried on climbing in the other direction. After a bit I glanced back; the man was stomping off now, leaving Megan sitting slumped on a rock, head hanging down. I circled back a little way; she was crying, for sure. *No, leave her alone, Kitty, it's none of your business*, I told myself. But I must have stood staring for a moment too long, because she looked up, glared at me and called out, 'What you looking at?' And then she told me to go away – only in much ruder terms.

I turned quickly, my face burning. *Blimey, no need to be so rude about it*, I thought. Trembling, I climbed on towards the headland. I felt insulted, but at the same time I couldn't shake the sympathy I'd felt for her a moment before. I felt really uncomfortable about the scene I'd witnessed. Just what had Megan got herself into? I had to admit, I was dying to know more. I'd have to tell Ashley about it. I didn't suppose she'd have much more of an idea as to what was going on, and there was no telling how she'd react. But I didn't feel I could ignore it.

But much as the Megan situation bothered me, I was frankly a bit more bothered about my own fate; the memory of the *Venus* soon came lurching back, repeating on me like a dodgy takeaway. Crossing the

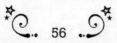

headland, I reached the point where I could see right over the cliff edge – but no sign of 'Jane Doe' anywhere. I would have to work on connecting with her – oh, but it was impossible without a proper name! And gazing down into the cove, I thought for a dizzying moment how easy it would be for me to trip and fall, go hurtling right down onto the rocks below.

How terrifyingly easy.

*Blimey, Kitty,* I thought. *This is the* last *thing you should be doing, when at any moment you might have another sighting of the* Venus*! Dimwit.*

But that wasn't the only danger. Suddenly, I was aware of the swooshing sound of someone walking briskly behind me. God: the man in the leather coat…he'd seen me.

I'd witnessed something I shouldn't have.

I Knew Too Much.

And he was after me now.

Why didn't I think of that?

*Stupid!*

I looked back, and his dark figure came swiftly forward…

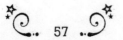

# Cut-throat Challenge

'Afternoon!' said the man, cheerily.

He was probably about sixty-five, and wearing a black windcheater – you know, one of those jackets that go *shush-shush-shush* as you walk. Hiking boots, chunky socks, nubbly wooden walking stick.

*Oh, thank god!*

I stepped back from the edge and nodded. 'Hi.'

Grey-haired wife was not far behind; she smiled and nodded. Just a nice old couple out for a brisk coastal walk of a spring day. Hallelujah.

And on they went, minding their own business. Leaving me to mind mine: Jane Doe. Now that it was so much clearer, I could see right over to the other side of Bosreath Cove. And it looked as if there might be a couple of really rough paths down to the beach. Only problem was: no beach – it was high tide. Still, it was

worth trying to get as far down as I could; it felt as if it was a more likely spot to find her. I walked round the bay, and took a closer look. The path was rough and steep; I started out on foot, but soon had to resort to doing the bum-slide, clinging on for dear life to tufts of grass as I went. Someone had chucked a Coke can down here; nice. The last few metres were just rough rocks, and beyond that, foamy turquoise waters sloshing around.

So now I got into channelling mode – well, as best I could. Down here with the blue-black cliffs towering over me, I was completely alone amid the roar of the sea. Finding a spot to perch on, I shut my eyes and concentrated hard on my ghost, my 'Jane Doe'.

Every now and then, I opened my eyes and looked around.

The cliffs jutted out overhead, grim-faced like green-tufted heads of giants, squinting in the wind. Gulls squealed overhead, and the air tasted of salt and seaweed. Across the bay was a huge black hole; a deep cave.

*Come on, Jane! Whoever you are!*

Something was drifting in the water; a buoy, I thought at first. No, hang on, not a buoy: it was an orange Sainsbury's bag. God, some people were morons, I thought; how hard was it just to take your rubbish home? Then I looked again: no, it wasn't orange; it was

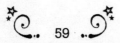

red. A red headscarf – *that* red headscarf – and it was attached to that head. Jane Doe was walking out of the water, and now here was her nose, her chin, her shoulders emerging…just walking straight ahead, unaffected by the foamy waters crashing all around her.

'Hello!' I cried.

She turned, and changed direction; she was coming towards me, and now her arms were free of the water. Yes! She must have heard me – she was looking straight at me now, and even though her expression didn't change, I felt we'd connected. I was getting to know the difference: so many ghosts I saw just went about their business, not taking any notice of me – it could be seriously frustrating at times. But there was a feeling I got when a connection was made, like a stream getting diverted and filling me up, and I got that feeling now. As she came nearer, I saw that her right hand was clenched tight; yes! Probably holding the medallion that Bill had mentioned. Surely this was her, my Jane Doe.

'Are you…?' I started, then realised there was no point asking if her name was Jane Doe. 'What's your name?' I asked.

She didn't answer; just looked me up and down, like I was an alien or something. Despite the fact that she'd just come out of the water, she looked grubby; her

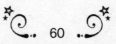

fingernails and toenails were black. But then I guessed ghost dirt didn't wash off. And she came from a time when people didn't wash very often.

I pointed to her clenched fist. 'What have you got there?'

'No!' she cried, yanking her arm away like a petulant child. 'Thee'm not 'avin' it. 'Smine!'

Whoah! The way she spoke threw me for a moment. 'No, no, it's OK! I don't want it!' I told her. 'I just want to know…it's the medal, isn't it? It belonged to Jed…Jed…' I couldn't remember his last name, but I saw the gleam in her eye as soon as I said 'Jed'.

'My Jed!' she cried, then thrust her face skyward. 'Aaurgh!'

It was an awful, guttural cry, and her face was contorted like a combination of happy and sad theatrical masks, both together. I didn't know what to say, so I just sat there and waited to see if she'd calm down.

Eventually she became quiet, and looked at me again. 'Do ee know him? Do ee know my Jed? Have ee seen 'im?'

'I…no,' I said. 'Sorry.'

'But ee lookin' to help me, ent ee? That's why thee'm here, idn' it?'

I was having some trouble understanding her accent

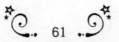

(especially with all those 'ee's: I kept thinking she was saying 'he'). But I got the general idea: she wanted *me* to help *her*. Um, wrong way round: I needed *her* to help *me* sort out this whole business with the *Venus* sightings. But what could I say? 'Well, yeah, I'll help any way I can, but—'

'All I be wantin' is my Jed back,' she said, leaning forward on the rock in front of me and staring me in the eye. 'He do make me cracky for all I's a-waitin'.'

Oh no. She wanted her dead lover back? There was no way I could help her with that! I really had to change the subject. 'I'm Kitty,' I said. 'What's your name?'

''Tis a secret,' she said.

'Your secret's safe with me,' I answered quickly. 'I promise. The truth is, I need your help too, so I'm not about to do anything to upset you.'

She gazed at me. 'You talk funny.'

'OK, but—'

' "OK, OK", what is "OK"?'

'Sorry. It's just something we...never mind. Look, I promise I won't tell anyone your name.' I crossed my heart.

She sniffed loudly and wiped her nose on her sleeve. 'Bath.'

'Bath?'

'Full name, 'Lizabath Trewin, of the Trewins of Charlestown.'

'Oh, *Beth*,' I said, understanding at last.

'Yur. Bath. There, now.'

'Why's it a secret?'

'Because my Jed an' I was in love, but I weren't allowed to see 'im, see? My pa did take on ghastly. He give me such a lacin' I couldn't take it no more…'

I listened hard. I wasn't sure what 'take on ghastly' or a 'lacin'' meant, but it definitely sounded like her dad didn't approve.

'…So I ran away after my Jed,' Beth went on. 'I were only five-an'-ten, but they'm din't know who I were on the ship, for I done went as the cabin boy, see? I were Charlie then; jus' Charlie, the cabin boy.'

'Oh, I see! So *that's* why you're dressed like that. And…this was on the *Venus*, right?' I prompted. I had to cut to the chase: I'd have to get back to the festival soon, or people would start to worry. 'What happened to the *Venus*, Beth?'

Her eyes turned all glassy. 'We was so close to home…so close! But he…*he* worked 'is evil magic. Such a terrible tempest as came out o' nowhere!' She got up and began pacing about in the water. 'So close…an' we knew these waters! Shouldn't never have happened!'

' "He"? Who's "he"?' I asked, hoping for more detail, but she was into a whole rant now.

'Even when I first felt the grindin' underneath, I'm be thinkin', "us'm come free, us'm come free"…but with the storm blowin', an' the rippin' of the sails…oh!'

She was going round in circles now, half crazed.

'Beth…'

She turned to me again, eyes blazing. 'All I wants is my Jed. Thee'm get 'im back for me! That's why thee'm here…'

*Er no, it isn't, actually*, I wanted to say. But trying to get a word in was like pushing back a tidal wave with a water pistol.

'Get me my Jed back!' demanded Beth.

'I…I'll try,' I said, even though I was sure she was asking the impossible.

All of a sudden, Beth whipped out a large knife, and aimed it under my chin. 'Tha *will*,' she growled.

The blade glinted at me. It couldn't cut me, could it? It was just an apparition, surely… All the same, I didn't find this reassuring. By now I'd learned enough about ghosts to know that you really didn't want to get on the wrong side of them. They could be a powerful force of nature.

'OK!' I said. 'Only…look, can we cut some sort of

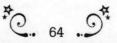

deal here? You see, that ship you were on, the *Venus*…it *was* the *Venus*, right?'

'Yar.'

'Well, the thing is, I saw it, right, and–'

The tip of the knife jabbed upwards: I felt a cold needling sensation. 'Thee'm get 'im back!' Beth repeated, even more fiercely.

'Yes! I *said*! Yes!' Then I realised that what I'd actually said before was "OK", which she obviously hadn't understood. 'Look, I've agreed to that part. It's just–'

But Beth wasn't listening. Suddenly, she threw her head back and howled with laughter. 'Oh yes!' she cried, now fixing me with that piercing stare of hers again.

My hopes of cutting any sort of deal with her were fast disappearing. By now I couldn't even figure out how to put it to her. I realised I'd have to explain all about the sightings, what had happened to people, what nearly happened to me… In any case, what control did she have over any of that? Plus, I was beginning to think she was crazy – and this time, not just ordinary everyday nice-but-slightly-bonkers, but stark raving loony-tune.

'T's in thy head now,' she said. 'And the sea's got in thee. Ent no escape.' Then she made a great swooping motion with the hand that held the knife; as she did so,

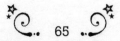

a trail of sea-foam followed it and enveloped her like a cloak. Then she and her watery cloak spun around, faster and faster, until she was transformed into a twisting sea-tornado, and off it spun into the distance, vanishing into the waves.

Amid the crashing of the waves and the cries of the gulls, I stood there with those words echoing in my brain: *I's in thy head now. And the sea's got in thee... Ent no escape...*

# Evil Magic

Great.

So now, as well as having the whole *Venus* omen thing to contend with, I'm in trouble with a mad ghost. Far from helping me unravel the story of the *Venus* and maybe – just MAYBE – getting me and/or future victims out of danger, I've gone and got myself into even deeper do-dos. Something tells me Beth Trewin's not going to let me off the hook on this one.

And it's a complete non-starter – how will I ever find Jed?

<u>The Body</u>

Location of someone's remains is the logical place to

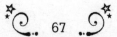

start, if you're looking for their spirit. BUT: no way am I EVER going to find Jed Lannion's body – OK, his bones. At the bottom of the sea somewhere. IMPOSSIBLE.

<u>The Spirit</u>

MIGHT be possible to reunite Beth with his spirit – but only if he's also haunting the mortal world with unfinished business of his own. How likely is that? Besides, they LOVE each other. Why wouldn't their spirits already have been united?

Nope, I reckon his spirit's gone over to the other side. So...WHAT is keeping her here?

OK: I'll just have to summon her again, tell her she's looking in the wrong place. Nothing I can do about that – end of story. That's what I should have said in the first place.

---

I told Ashley about Megan and the strange man; she didn't seem to care. 'If Megan's going to behave like an idiot, that's her choice,' she said. 'Nothing you can do.'

'Don't you think that's a bit harsh?'

Ashley sighed. 'Look, I really don't care about Megan. She used to bully me, if you must know; teased me about believing in pixies and stuff – even laughed at

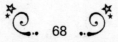

my singing, 'cause it was "uncool", or something.'

'But I think she might be in real danger!' I said. 'Don't you think that's a bit more important than some stupid bit of taunting back in primary school?'

'Look, yeah, she's probably involved in something illegal; I wouldn't be surprised. You want my advice? Don't stick your nose in where it's not wanted.'

And having doled out that sound little piece of advice, she went on to stick *her* nose in about my phantorama, and any other ghosts I might have seen.

Well, I didn't tell her about Beth Trewin: didn't feel like it.

I was quite glad that she'd be going back to school the next day; I really needed a bit of time away from her.

All the same, I badly wanted to tell *someone*: this was too big to keep all bottled up. I needed some help in making sense of it all. Basically, I needed to talk to Sam and Floss, before I went completely nuts myself.

I finally got my chance late that night. Maro took herself off to bed early, muttering something about being tired from all the sea air. Sam, Floss and I had a conference under a clear black glittering sky, sitting on the Giants' Quoits.

'Listen, something really freaky happened today, and I think it's about time we did some investigating,' I said,

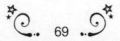

then thought for a moment. 'Actually, two things happened.'

'OK, what was the first thing?' asked Sam.

So I spilled out the whole story about what Bill had told me, and what had happened with Beth Trewin. 'I thought I was really onto something when I found out that she was actually a crew member on the *Venus*. I reckon that the best way to get to the bottom of exactly what happened to those people who had the visions before me – and why – is to find out all we can about that ship, its crew…anything connected to it. But then it was frustrating, 'cause I couldn't get a word in edgeways with Beth; all she did was nag me to find her boyfriend.'

'Do you think you can help her?' asked Flossie.

'Not likely,' I said. 'Oh, by the way, Maro can't know about any of this. Are we agreed on that?'

'Agreed.'

'Agreed.'

'Right,' I said. 'We don't want her worrying unnecessarily. Or stopping us doing any investigating she might think is dangerous.'

'But…there *isn't* any danger, right?' said Flossie, nervously. 'I can't stop thinking about that bad omen…'

'Floss, I told you, you mustn't worry about that,'

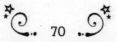

I said. 'And right now, all we're talking about is a bit of research. But there's no need to tell Maro. This is our Golden Rule from now on. It's kind of how we've been operating, but we haven't made it a rule till now. Oh, and part two of the Golden Rule is, the same goes for any other adults involved.'

'Does Ty count as an adult?' asked Flossie.

"Course he does,' said Sam. 'But Kitty, Maro was very suspicious when you went AWOL today. She's not stupid, you know.'

'I know. That's why I'm going to "confess" to some other ghostly encounter…don't worry, I've got it all figured out. And Aunt Phoebe's gonna know about the phantorama sooner or later anyway. But she'll get the same story I feed Maro. I'm not having them thinking I might get lured off a cliff at any moment…' Flossie's eyes widened in alarm, so I quickly added, '…which *isn't* going to happen, of course, Floss. It's like I said: the omen didn't work in my case, because of my phantorama.'

'Yeah, I know you said that, but–'

'It's true, Floss,' said Sam. 'Kitty just wants to get to the bottom of this so she can stop it happening to other people – right, Kit?'

'Right. I mean, Floss, just think of the lives I could save, if I lifted this curse! After all, I've done it before.'

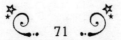

'Oh, right!' said Flossie. 'Wow. That would be a pretty amazing thing to do. God, I'm so glad you're immune!'

I smiled and nodded. *Yeah, I'm immune! Keep telling yourself that, Kitty...*

'So...what do we do?' asked Flossie.

'Well, the first thing is really down to me and Sam,' I said. 'You see, tomorrow we start the diving course. And apparently this theory work we're doing for the first couple of days is done in the local library. So, Sam, what I'm thinking is, how about we look stuff up in the lunch break?'

'Oh yeah, good idea,' said Sam.

'We'll start with the *Venus*,' I said. 'Then see what we can find out about Beth Trewin.'

'Where d'you say she was from?' asked Sam.

'Charlestown. It's right near Plymouth – I looked it up on the map. Oh, and there's her boyfriend, Jed Lannion; let's see what we can find out about him, too. There's also someone else, but I don't know what chance we have of finding out about that. Someone Beth said was working his "evil magic". Didn't make much sense, to be honest – it was like she was saying he had...something to do with causing the storm that sank the ship? I dunno, like I say, she's kind of bonkers. But anyway: Beth Trewin and Jed Lannion.'

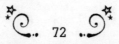

'OK,' said Sam.

'So there's nothing for me to do, then,' said Flossie.

'Oh no, there is,' I said. 'You can help me by…just observing things a little bit. Because there's this other thing that happened today I haven't told you about yet.' I told them about what I'd witnessed with Megan and the man who'd been harassing her.

'Oh, *her*,' said Sam. 'Hey, I think I saw her with her gang – must've been just after you did. Does she have dreadlocks with bits of pink in them?'

'Yeah, that's her,' I said. 'Thing is, Ashley's no help. She just thinks anything bad that happens to Megan is her own stupid fault, and it's none of our business.'

'I think she's right,' said Flossie. 'It *isn't* any of our business.'

I chewed my lip. 'Sam?'

'I think we've got our hands full with the *Venus* and the dead people, if you must know,' said Sam.

'OK, OK, but…still, it bothers me. Just be aware, OK? Keep your eyes and ears open for any clues. I mean, what if something really bad happened to her – something that could have been prevented? I'd feel terrible!'

The book's title made my heart lurch:

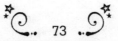

THE
# CURSE
OF THE
# VENUS

It was a ragged-looking old booklet, with a plain off-white cover, and kind of wonky print. We found it in the library's 'local information' corner, which was packed with stuff you'd never in a million years find anywhere else. Books on Cornish shipwrecks, pamphlets just on shipwrecks in the Pelporth area...and *The Curse of the Venus*.

Underneath the title was a not-very-good line drawing of the ship – which I recognised instantly as the same one I'd seen that day in Pelporth harbour. 'Oh, right,' I said as Sam handed the booklet to me. My mouth was suddenly as dry as paper. 'Yup, that'll, um... That'll be it.'

I thumbed through it. Here and there were grainy black-and-white photographs of some of the people who had come to a grisly end: Norman Cavendish, Harriet Jenkins...

'Wow,' said Sam, looking over my shoulder. 'Ashley knew it all off by heart, didn't she? There's the eighties woman...the man from the 1950s...'

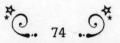

'Yup. And look: the names go all the way back to the 18th century: there's nine of them in all.'

'Yes, and...hmm. They seem to be pretty evenly spaced, too,' said Sam. 'Looks like there's one roughly every thirty years.'

'And the last one was, um...' I swallowed hard. '1982.'

I looked at Sam. Sam looked at me.

'Well, yes, but that doesn't mean...' He trailed off.

'Oh no? That's thirty years ago, Sam. There's another one due right around now.'

Sam took the booklet from my hands. 'Yes, well, the whole thing's a bunch of baloney anyway.' He turned to the back, where there was information about the author. 'Who is this guy? Probably some nutcase! If anyone took this remotely seriously it'd be in the papers and everything – 'specially now.'

I forced myself to calm down. 'OK, well...there's not much info on the actual ship, anyway.' I pulled out a book on Cornish shipwrecks, and looked up the *Venus*. 'This is more like it, look: "The *Venus*: an East Indiaman privateer ship captained by Zachary Quaid, sank off the coast at Pelporth, April 6th, 1728... What's an East Indiaman privateer ship?"

'I think "East Indiaman" is the type of ship,' said Sam,

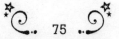

flipping through the pages. "'Cause look: there's another one, and another one.'

'And "privateer"?'

'Erm, not sure... Is there anything in there about Beth Trewin?'

'No – but then there wouldn't be. She was in disguise, remember? As Charlie, the cabin boy. I didn't even get a last name for him. We have to look her up in other books...'

'Like, which ones?'

'Um...' I scanned the shelves, but nothing looked promising.

'You know what I don't quite get?' said Sam. 'Beth ran away, right? Well, wasn't she ever reported missing?'

'Erm...well, yeah, you'd think she would be, wouldn't you? For that matter, why didn't anyone ever link her to this Jane Doe that was found?'

'Yeah...could there have been something about the body that made them rule that out, d'you think?' said Sam.

'Hmm... Well, I guess her appearance might have changed, but even so...I dunno. I'll have to think about it some more. I wonder how long she was at sea? She ran away at 15...she can't have been much older when she died, judging by the look of her ghost.'

'OK, well…what about Lannion?" said Sam.

'He's mentioned…but all it says is that he was 21 when the ship went down. Zachary Quaid was 50. Oh, but we must be able to find out more about *him*, at least!'

Sam glanced at the clock. 'Oops, we're meant to be back in class. C'mon!'

'So how was diving class?' asked Ashley, when we got home.

'Oh, good, thanks,' I said, helping myself to some biscuits from the cupboard. I didn't mention our bit of lunchtime research, as I didn't feel like telling her about Beth. The way she'd behaved about that girl Megan was still bugging me; I wasn't in the mood.

'You must be looking forward to the actual diving part,' said Ashley.

'Yeah, I am. It's almost like they want to put you off it, though – you know, drumming it into you about all the things that can go wrong. But I'm not scared.'

'Ah, hello Kitty,' said Uncle Sean, as he came in. 'What's this – diving class? Did you enjoy it?'

'Yes, thanks. Bit nervous about going down the first time, but…no, it's exciting!'

'Good!' said Sean, fetching himself a glass of water. 'You'll be fine.'

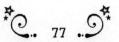

'Oh, Uncle Sean? What's a privateer ship?'

'Privateer ship? Oh, those were merchant ships, going back to the seventeenth, eighteenth centuries – but ones that were used at times of war. They were sent out to raid other merchant ships belonging to the enemy.'

'*Raid* them?'

'Yes, you know: remove any valuables.'

One of the family cats, Minnie, came over and started sniffing around my legs. I rubbed her under the chin. 'What, like pirates, you mean?'

'Ha ha! Well, yes, in a way. But unlike pirates, the privateers weren't criminals, because they were actually sent out by the government to do the raids. Seize the enemy's assets. It was totally above board. Well, usually.'

The cat was sniffing around my legs, like I was hiding some food in my socks or something. 'What do you mean, "usually"?' I asked, shifting away. It did not deter her.

'Well, some privateers were less scrupulous–'

'What's that smell?' interrupted Ashley, sniffing the air around me.

Sean shot her a look. 'Ashley! Don't be so rude!' He turned back to me. 'Yes, there were some privateers who didn't always hand over all the spoils…you OK there?

Minnie! Psst!' He tried shooing away the cat, who was really starting to annoy me, licking my leg and making little purry-miaow noises.

'I'm not being funny,' said Ashley, 'but there really is a sort of…fishy smell.'

'We're not having fish tonight,' said Sean. 'Why do you ask, Kitty?'

'Hmm?'

'About the privateer ships.'

'Oh, it's just…since we were out looking at that shipwreck the other day, I've got really interested in the subject,' I said. 'And I was reading about this one called the *Venus,* that sank without trace?'

'Ark!' cried Winston the cockatoo, as he flew in from the living room, and landed on Sean's hand. 'Hello, Winston,' said Sean. 'The *Venus*: yes, I know about that one. Long time ago – eighteenth century.'

'I think it's amazing that the wreck has never been found in all that time. How can that be?'

'Well, you see, a ship can drift for miles once it's been fatally damaged.'

I still found it hard to believe. 'People must have gone looking for it though, right? Like those guys we saw the other day, the ones that go diving for treasure? Don't they go looking for lost ships as well?'

Sean shook his head. 'No: not generally speaking, anyway. Like I say, they're mostly tourists. They tend to stick to the locations of known wrecks. Even though loads of others will have gone before them, you'd be amazed what people can still find. I heard of someone finding some gold coins, just the other day! But for lost ships…you'd have to be some sort of specialist…' He trailed off and looked at Ashley, who was frowning, and sniffing loudly.

'I'm sorry, but there really is a fishy smell,' she said. 'Where's it coming from?'

'I have no idea, Ashley,' said Sean.

The cat was really starting to bug me now; circling my feet, all agitated, and miaowing. And now the other two were joining her. What with the cats and the bird, there was quite a commotion now; I had to raise my voice to make myself heard. 'SO WHAT ABOUT THESE SPECIALISTS, THEN?' I said. 'DON'T *THEY* GO OUT AND FIND MISSING SHIPS?'

'Sometimes, yes,' said Sean. 'Often many years later. Decades…centuries, even. Only with the older ones, the wooden ones, they wouldn't find the actual ship itself. The timbers rot away, you see. You'd just get valuables, cannon…maybe a ship's bell…'

'Ark!' cried Winston; he swooped over and landed on my head.

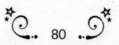

'Aah!' I cried, as he pecked at my hair.

'Shoo, Winston!' said Ashley, waving him away. 'Hey – what's this?'

I felt something slip from my head, as if I'd had a hairband on or something.

Ashley pulled, and out came a long, rubbery ribbon of seaweed.

I blinked at it. 'How the hell did that get there?'

I looked at Ashley. Ashley looked at me. I was speechless. And all I could think of was Beth Trewin, and her warning: 'the sea's got in thee'. Oh wow. What had I got myself into now?

# Captain Quaid

*I'm in a cramped, gloomy little room, and my father's looming over me, furious. And he's shouting, red-faced. Why isn't supper ready? Why hasn't the hearth been swept, or the washing been taken in? Where've I been?*

*So I mutter something…don't worry, I'm doing it now…thinking, hurry, hurry…mustn't keep him waiting, he'll go mad…*

*Then, whack! He hits me across my head. I stumble sideways.*

*No, Pa, please, I'm sorry!*

*Thwack! Another blow, knocking me to the floor…*

*Now it's night; I am alone. This is it, I tell myself, as I pull on my shirt and trousers. I won't put up with this any more. Twisting my hair up tightly, I hold it in place with my ivory comb, then cover my head with my red scarf: there, I say to*

*myself in the mirror:* good lad. *I gather up my few belongings and creep out. My father is snoring…he doesn't hear. I'm free – for now. But I won't be truly safe until I'm away on that boat…he'll kill me if he finds out. The moon is high in the sky as I make my way down to the harbour; I'm filled with excitement as the masts of the* Venus *come into view….*

*Dawn. The lines are untied; the ship begins to ease out of the harbour. I feel the gentle rolling movement beneath me, breathe in the cold salt air. They didn't give me a second glance as I signed in; I am Charlie Pentland now. I'm free from my father! He can't hurt me now. And here's my Jed, my lovely Jed – not smiling at me, just the barest glance. Got to be careful. But nothing's going to stop us now, me and my Jed…*

I jolted awake. Where was I? *Who* was I? For a few seconds I literally didn't know. It was the freakiest sensation.

I gasped, made a sudden movement – enough to wake Flossie. 'What is it?' she asked.

'God, I just had this dream…'

'Urgh.' Flossie flopped over onto her other side, annoyed.

'No, listen, Floss, I gotta tell you about this! It's not like anything else I've ever experienced…it was the

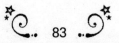

ghost, Beth Trewin, right, and she was in my head, so that…Floss, I *was* Beth Trewin!'

'Whaddaya mean, you *were* her?'

'God it was so real…it's still with me now. I was dreaming scenes from her life, Floss! It's like I was actually inside her head!'

'Hold on, I'm confused,' said Flossie. 'Was she in your head, or were you in hers?'

'I was in hers…well, except, in order for me to get there, she had to get into mine first…oh, never mind! The point is that it was as if all this stuff was happening to me. I saw what she saw, in loads of detail!'

I told Floss the whole story; I described the fury I'd seen in 'my' dad's face, the masts of the *Venus* against the grey dawn…everything. 'But the main thing was how I felt all Beth's emotions: fear, anger…then there was the hope, and the love for Jed.'

'Didja see him?' asked Floss.

'Yes, right at the end…'

'Was he nice?'

'Yeah, he was pretty good-looking…nice, kind face. Dark hair, blue eyes…kind of weathered. God, it's just amazing…I never thought this was possible! It's like she was showing me a movie, almost. She *told* me this would happen, "I's in thy head" that's what she said.

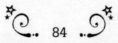

Blimey, she wasn't kidding.'

'Only except *you* were in *her* head...'

'OK, OK, whatever...question is, why'd she need to do it this way? Like, instead of just telling me what happened, I mean?'

'Because she wanted to show you Jed?' suggested Flossie.

'Well, yeah...I guess, since she wants me to "find" him. Which I'm never going to be able to do.'

'You could try,' said Flossie.

'Guess I should. But how?' I sighed. We sat in silence.

'Wow,' said Flossie. 'Imagine running off to sea like that, only fifteen!'

'Not to mention pretending to be a boy,' I said. 'I mean, can you imagine trying to keep that up? For, like – well, I don't know how long. Probably years! I'd have a hard time doing it for a *day*.'

Flossie giggled.

'Will you guys shut up?' groaned Sam from his bed on the other side of the Hippo.

'Sorry,' I said. I turned to Flossie. 'G'night.'

'Uh-huh,' said Flossie. 'Y'know, Kitty?'

'What?'

'That Beth, she must have been really brave.'

'Yeah,' I said. 'I reckon she was. I *felt* that, you know?

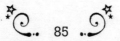

Not to mention the desperation. I felt how scared she was of her dad, how much she hated him. He was a cruel man, for sure. Actually...'

'What?'

'Oh, it's just that...one thing that's been bugging me, is why he apparently didn't report her missing. But then, he probably figured out what she'd done, didn't he? But couldn't do anything about it – yet. He probably thought, "I'll just wait till the ship returns then I'll nab her."'

'Mm...probably,' said Flossie, yawning. She turned over and went back to sleep.

I stared into the darkness, thinking. I still couldn't get over the experience of that dream: I knew it was going to stay with me for days. But did it tell me anything useful about the *Venus*? Not really. Not yet, anyway: I had a feeling I'd only experienced the first instalment of this story. There would be more to come...

A couple of days later we dived. It was cool, but we didn't get to go down very deep or see all that much. There's all this stuff you have to remember to do with your equipment, and blowing your nose so your ears don't pop and everything. But then you reach your ten

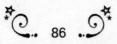

metres or whatever and you just sort of hang there, weighted just enough so's you don't float up and it's like you're an astronaut in open space. *Really* cool, actually. Hey, but I didn't see any ghosts. Plenty of pretty seaweed (that surprised me; never thought of seaweed as being pretty before). Some starfish, and sponges…no ghosts.

And the one I really wanted to see now was of course Jed Lannion – just because if by some complete miracle I managed to connect with him, that might make Beth help me out with this whole *Venus* business. So after we'd gone back to the house I scooted out to a quiet spot so I could try and channel him. I sat on one of the lichen-covered stones, the Giants' Quoits, closed my eyes and summoned up a picture of him in my head, just as I'd seen him in the dream. And I said his name over and over again to myself. *Beth is calling you!* I told him. *Can't you hear?*

Nothing.

Oh, this was ridiculous. Beth had already been calling to him for two hundred and fifty years! Why the hell would he respond to me, now, when he'd been ignoring her all this time? Well, either he *was* ignoring her deliberately, or else he couldn't actually hear her. Or me.

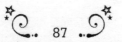

Argh…

I wandered back to the Hippo, thinking…

---

**GHOST BLOG**

**THURSDAY 5 MAY**

OK, something doesn't add up here.

Beth and Jed died together on the sinking ship. They were in love. IN LURRV. Well, for god's sake, why weren't their spirits united for all eternity??! Isn't that what happens? I mean, it COULD be that the whole dying-and-being-reunited-with-your-loved-ones thing is just one great big con – I don't know, do I? But it just doesn't make SENSE that Beth is trapped here in the mortal world, while Jed has 'gone over to the other side', as they say. He must have done: there's no other explanation. Her unfinished business, the thing that's keeping her here, is finding Jed – but why does she have to search for him?

SOMETHING MUST HAVE HAPPENED TO COME BETWEEN THEM.

Or –

Maybe Jed Lannion went off Beth, because she was a bit crazy?? So by the time of the shipwreck, he was

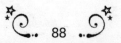

like, get me AWAY from this woman, only there was no escape, 'cause he was stuck on the ship with her. Death, though: THAT was a way out. Except SHE was still in love with HIM: no way would she not have followed him.

Hmm.

No, there's more to this, I'm sure – stuff I don't know yet. Like, what caused the ship to sink? If I can find that out, then maybe I can get to the bottom of this whole horrible curse business. NO idea how I can help Beth, though….and I swear she's wasting her time searching for Jed. Or wasting whatever it is that ghosts have instead of time. Abstract energy. But how the hell am I going to convince her of that? How can I tell her to give up? It would be like telling a dog to stop chasing rabbits.

---

*The stars are clear tonight. A beautiful night: just a soft breeze, the gentle rocking of the ship, the creaking of the rigging. A night for lovers, if ever there was one. Cool air on my face, the fire of wine in my belly, the thrill of a secret glance from Jed; he winks. Oh, how I want to cuddle up to him!*

*But I can't.*

*Most of the men are up here on deck; soft voices, an accordion playing…someone tells a joke: laughter. Pass the*

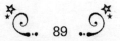

*wine. Jed tips the flagon upside-down: Aah, we're all out.*
*He turns to me: Charlie, fetch us some more from the galley,*
*there's a lad.*

*I take the empty flagon and go down. I've just refilled it,*
*when I turn and find Jed right there, in front of me. He's*
*found some excuse, and followed me. He smiles, pulls me*
*towards him. And down here, with no one around, our secret*
*is safe: we steal a kiss. I'm in heaven. My Jed! He is my whole*
*world…*

*Slam! The galley door smacks against the panelled wall.*
*Well, what have we here, then, eh?*

*Captain Quaid.*

*We jump apart, but it is too late; he knows. For two whole*
*years, we've kept our love a secret, and now…oh, how could*
*we have been so careless!*

*Quaid grabs my face roughly, and tilts it towards him.*
*God, he's ugly! That's not a nose, it's a snout, with its two*
*cavernous nostrils jutting out of that fat, greasy, bearded face.*
*I can smell the rotting flesh of his gouty leg. He pulls off my*
*headscarf; my sweat-stiffened curls unbend themselves, and*
*my comb falls to the ground.*

*A girl, eh? And a fair one, at that.*

*Peeeeep! He blows his whistle, and in no time the men are*
*there. Strap 'im up for a keelhauling, he says, nodding at Jed.*
*Then cut him loose!*

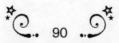

*Jed is led out, struggling… No! Jed! I scream, but the captain has me like a vice in his meaty hands.*

*As for you, my dear, he says. You'll do just handsome as a captain's bride; I'm tired o' being a bachelor!*

*Not on your life! I cry, pulling away.*

*Ah, but you see, he says, you don't really have a say in the matter, my lovely. Besides, I'm well on my way to becoming a wealthy man, did you know that? Very wealthy.*

*He reaches into his pocket, pulls out a sparkling diamond and holds it up to my face between his thumb and forefinger. See this? he says. Worth ten guineas all by itself. You know how many more we got down in the hold? Hundreds. An' pearls as well; bags an' bags of 'em!*

*But they's not yours, I say. You got to hand over when we get home.*

*Quaid laughs his gravel laugh. You don't know me very well, do you? Oh, sure, the commissioner'll get his cut. But he'll never know the full amount. Trust me: I'm to be a very wealthy man. So, he says, pocketing the diamond again. How's about a kiss now, eh? He leans in with his filthy dog-breath; I wriggle like crazy, but I feel like an octopus's dinner. I'm leaning backwards, and my free hand searches the table behind me…here's a pewter beer-pot. I hook my little finger round the handle, pull it towards me…*

*And–*

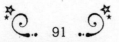

*Now!*

*I smack the half-full pot at his head; stale beer sloshes out, and I feel his grip loosen so I bring up my knee and kick at him with all my might. He laughs as he stumbles, then he's after me again…I thrust my hands into a sack of dried peas, throw them across the galley floor. His feet give way under him and crack! His head hits the corner of the table–*

*Everything slows down…*

*And he slumps into a heap. And he isn't moving…*

*Jed? I call, backing towards the door. Jed!*

'Aah!' I woke up in the Hippo, streaming with sweat. I hadn't meant to fall asleep; I guessed I was just tired from the diving, and not enough sleep the night before. And now, even though I knew I was myself again, I still felt stained by the dream. The horror, the shame… I knew that the Captain lay dead from his injury.

But what happened next?

What happened to Jed? Was he tortured and killed, like the captain instructed? Maybe *that* had something to do with why their souls were never united. Or did he escape that fate somehow? What happened to Beth, for that matter? Was she punished? OK, so technically the captain's death wasn't her fault, but only she knew that. It certainly wouldn't have looked very good – and she

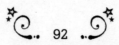

had a motive, after all. What would the rest of the crew have made of it? And what happened to those jewels?

So many unanswered questions: I *had* to know more! And find out exactly what it was that had caused the apparitions of the *Venus*, and all those deaths…

# A Bit Fishy

'Hey, Sam.'

No reaction. We'd just had our second day of diving, and were on the boat heading back to the harbour. Sam was gazing through a pair of binoculars.

'Sam!'

'Oh, hi,' said Sam, glancing at me before turning back to the binoculars. 'You should check these out, they're so cool! Dead powerful. I just saw some seals.'

'Uh-huh. Hey, Sam, I didn't get a chance to talk to you yet–'

Sam looked at me properly. 'What? Is something up?'

'No, well, yeah…it's just, I had another one of those dreams.' I filled him in on the latest episode, about Captain Quaid discovering Beth was a girl, the diamonds and pearls he boasted about, Beth's struggle with

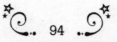

him…how he'd fallen to his death.

'Wow, that's some story,' said Sam. 'So I guess Quaid was planning to keep those jewels for himself, then?'

'Yeah – some of them, anyway. Said the "commissioner" would never know. I guess that would be the government person he was s'posed to hand them over to. Honestly, it's disgusting! It's like he was trying to *buy* Beth as a wife. And she was young enough to be his daughter!'

'Gross,' said Sam. 'So he didn't go down with the ship when it sank, then.'

'Oh yeah, I guess not. That book we saw in the library thought he did, but I guess they just assumed.'

'And what about the jewels? What happened to them?'

I shrugged. 'I don't know. Can't get a handle on what happened exactly when. But I guess there's a good chance they went down with the ship.'

'Wow, that would be some find, man!' Sam peered through the binoculars again. 'So…the captain dying: is that the reason for these weird apparitions, then – the sightings of the ship?'

'I've been asking myself the same question,' I said. 'But…how would that be?'

'Hmm.'

'I don't know what to think. I guess all this new info should help somehow, but...*pfft*. I'm not getting it.'

'Huh, that's weird,' said Sam, lowering his binoculars.

'I know.'

'No, not that. You know that girl, the one with the dreadlocky hair? Megan, was it?'

'Yeah; what about her?'

'I could swear I just saw her on that beach over there. Here,' he said, handing me the binoculars. 'What do you think?'

As I looked through the binoculars, Sam guided them so they pointed towards a deserted cove. 'See? Is that her?'

I could see a lone figure walking across the beach, but it wasn't clear; I focused in on her. 'Oh yeah! That's her, all right. Wow. Well spotted, Sam.' The cove was steeply enclosed on all sides; it was hard to figure out how anyone could get there. But Megan had, and now she was heading towards the cliff face, where she soon disappeared into shadow. I squinted up at the cliffs. 'Is that a cave there, d'you reckon?' I asked, passing back the glasses.

Sam peered through. 'Hard to tell...oh, is that where she went? Guess it must be; hard to make out.'

I pointed to the cove, and spoke to the instructor:

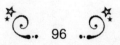

'What's that cove over there?'

'That place? Doesn't have a name,' he said. 'It's inaccessible.'

'It can't be,' said Sam. 'We just saw someone there.'

'Really? Huh.' He shrugged. 'Well, people do crazy things sometimes, end up having to be rescued by helicopters. Don't you go getting any ideas!' He started up the engine.

I kept watching until the cove disappeared from view, but didn't see Megan after that – nor anyone else, for that matter. I half expected to see the man in the leather coat; I couldn't help wondering if he had something to do with why she was there. Well, 'inaccessible' the cove might be, but it wasn't very far from the village; we passed just one more small inlet before coming to Bosreath Cove. God, this was annoying; now I was more curious than ever!

Later on, we met up with Ashley and some of her schoolfriends at the Lobster Pot Café in the village. Steamy little place decorated with seashells and all that corny Cornwall stuff. It's where they hang out after school on a Friday. We asked them about the little cove.

'Oh, I know the place you mean,' said Ashley.

'You do?' I said.

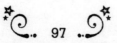

'Isn't that the one where there's supposed to be some tunnel?' said one of the other girls. 'You can actually get there, apparently – if you know the deal.'

'I thought everyone knew that place,' said Oliver. 'I haven't been, but my brother went to a party there once.'

'How old's your brother?' I asked.

'Seventeen. Well, I don't think it was much of a party, really. They just sort of hung out there for a bit – for kicks, you know. It used to be a smugglers' den.'

'I knew that!' Ashley practically shrieked. Oliver's coolness rating among the group had just been upped several notches, and she seemed desperate to link herself to him, and have some of the coolness rub off on her.

'Really?' I said. 'What, they used to store stuff in caves there?'

'Yeah,' said Oliver. 'Brilliant spot for it, 'cause it was really hard for the tax men to get to.'

'What kind of things did they smuggle in?' asked Sam.

'Oh, tea, coffee, gin…' said Oliver.

'Whisky, gin,' added Ashley, not actually adding anything at all.

'It was dangerous,' Oliver went on, ignoring her, 'cause they had to bring the ships in at night, with no lights–'

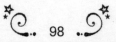

'Yeah, it was *really* dangerous,' punctuated Ashley.

'But they could make a lot of money selling the stuff on the black…market.' Oliver trailed off. He was looking at me, and apparently something was bothering him.

'Uh-huh,' I said, hoping he would move on. But he didn't, and now some of the others were also giving me strange looks. At the same time, I became aware of a dampness around my neck and under my arms. Then there was a wriggling sensation in my left sleeve, as if…as if something live was caught in there.

An awful, clammy embarrassment welled up inside me as I realised it was happening again, like with the seaweed that time back at the house. I had to get out of there! I glanced at the clock, gasped, 'Oh god, is that the time?' and slammed down my mug. As I did so, a pilchard slithered out of my sleeve and plopped onto the table. Yes: a real live, silvery fish, flipping madly among the mugs and glasses and napkins.

'Aah!' someone squealed; then everything went quiet.

*Plip, plop, plip.*

It was the only sound in the whole place.

And then I spotted a hunched figure, sitting alone at the corner table. The figure turned to face me, eyes glinting, and I saw the red headscarf and the pockmarked

face of Beth Trewin. She threw back her head and cackled loudly. Then she shimmered into nothingness.

Meanwhile, there was me, and there was the fish. *Plip, plop.*

And finally, after what felt like a week but was probably, like, *seconds*, Sam clapped his hands and let out a roar of laughter. 'Oh, Kitty, that's your best trick yet! Excellent!'

I watched as Oliver scooped the fish into a glass of water.

'Trick…' I said blankly, still basically in a state of shock. Then I realised what Sam was doing: helping me to save face. 'Trick…yeah. Ha ha! Good, eh?'

Everyone laughed – well, everyone except Ashley.

'Oh wow, that's, er…brilliant!' said Oliver, wiping his hand dry before joining in the applause. 'How d'you *do* that?' He was clearly impressed – though, I reckoned, a bit spooked at the same time.

Ashley's face crumpled. She opened her mouth like she was about to say something – like, 'Guess what, it's not a trick, Kitty's actually deeply weird!' But then she seemed to realise it would be impossible to explain without having to mention my phantorama. And *that*, no doubt, would only get me more admiration from Oliver, not less.

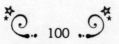

Ashley's mouth was soon shut again.

'OK, *what* was going on back there?' asked Ashley, after we'd got well away from the Lobster Pot.

'Ghost magic, apparently,' I said. 'And the ghost's name is Beth Trewin – AKA Jane Doe. *That* Jane Doe, the one Bill was telling us about; I found out all about her.'

'Oh.' Ashley was dumbfounded for a moment. 'Well, don't bother to tell me, or anything.'

'Yeah, well, I didn't tell you because I was annoyed with you, if you must know.'

'What? Why?'

I sighed. 'I nearly told you, but then I was trying to warn you about Megan being in trouble, and, well, frankly I think your attitude to her stinks.'

'Ha! What do you know?' cried Ashley. 'You have no idea how mean she was to me, and how she–'

'No, you're right, I don't know,' I interrupted. 'And you know what? I don't *care*. Because you just have to get over yourself. God, listen to you! You're not in primary school any more.'

'It's not just that!' snapped Ashley. 'She's just a scumbag; that lot are the lowest of the low–'

'Yeah,' I said, 'and I bet plenty of people would have said the same thing about Beth Trewin.'

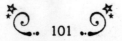

'I don't know about her.'

'Well, let me tell you. She went away to sea, disguised as a boy – when she was only fifteen, same age as Megan. She was in love with a sailor, but she also wanted to escape her home, where her dad treated her horribly. He used to beat her–'

'Oh, no way does Bill beat Megan!' protested Ashley.

'I'm not saying he does! Let me finish!' I took a deep breath. 'Look: all I'm saying is, sometimes people do bad things because they feel they have no choice – maybe because they're poor like Megan, maybe because they're treated badly. Beth even killed her captain! Well, not literally…but you could say she was responsible for his death. He'd just ordered her boyfriend to be killed, and wanted her for himself. I saw it all happen with my own eyes! I *felt* what *she* felt, and…and you know what? I understood how she…' I could feel the emotion rise in my throat, and next thing I knew, I was sobbing.

'I don't understand,' said Ashley. 'None of this makes any sense.'

Sam had been keeping his distance behind us while we were arguing, but he walked over now. 'Kitty's been having these dreams,' he explained. He told her about the encounter I'd had with Beth Trewin, about how crazed she was over losing Jed, and how she'd insisted

I must be able to help. 'She told her, "I's in thy head";
that's when Kitty started getting these dreams of
Beth's life.'

'Yeah,' I said, sniffing. 'And it was like I *was* her; it
was all so real! And the seaweed, and the fish? That's
her way of taunting me. I saw her there, in the Lobster
Pot, laughing at me. She's crazy, and I just know she
won't stop this until I get her Jed back for her. Which
I can't.'

'Oh.'

The wind buffeted our hair about as we sat by the
path, thinking.

I took out a tissue and blew my nose. 'Look. You
already know I've seen the *Venus*. To be honest, I'm a bit
more freaked out about that than I am about having
the odd pilchard drop out of my sleeve. But Beth, the
*Venus*…they're part of the same story. All I can hope to
do is piece together what happened on that ship…
maybe even find what's left of it.'

'Maybe you'll dream some more,' said Ashley.

'I can't just rely on that. I've got to investigate every
possible angle. That cove: I think we should go there.
I don't know…I was just thinking that if it was a famous
smuggling cove, maybe there's a connection to the
*Venus*. I mean, it was a merchant ship, so…you never

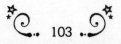

know. Maybe they were planning to smuggle some stuff in.'

'Hmm...'

'OK, so it's a long shot, but no one's ever found the ship's wreck, don't forget. I need to do all the exploring I can. Anyway, there's another reason I want to go there...I didn't mention it back there in the café, but Sam and I saw Megan there today.'

'You did?'

'From the boat,' explained Sam. 'We had binoculars.'

'So who knows?' I said. 'We might even get to the bottom of what's going on with her as well. Can you help me with that, Ashley...can you?'

# No-go Zone

*I'm with my husband, Captain Jed Lannion. Here we are, in his cabin, plotting our course on the map. Look, he says; we'll be home afore the next moon. I rest my head on his shoulder and sneak a look in the glass: we make a fine-looking couple. Even finer when we get home with all these riches. Imagine the wonderful things we'll have then! Clothes of lace and silk, a table laden with roasted meats…oh, how long since I tasted fresh meat! My taste buds tingle at the thought. And all served up by servants, with the finest linen and crystal and silver…*

*Do I feel guilty? No. We've had a tough life, Jed and me. Everyone hated Captain Quaid – they were only too glad he was dead. Captain Lannion is so much more liked.*

*Jed? I say. – Yes, my love. – He won't find me, will he? My father? I do think he might kill me for running away like that.*

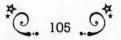

*You're safe with me. You're Charlotte now: Charlotte Lannion. And just look at you! You're a lean colt now – a palomino, with your bleached hair. And your scars just make you more beautiful to me; every one has a tale to tell.*

*Safe! And happy. And oh so near to home now...*

*It's late. And it's getting dark. We thought we'd be home by now, but the wind's turned. All hands are on board, and I'm helping too, trying to steer a course well wide of the reef. But the wind is whipping up hard.*

*Pull. That way. Pull...harder! Rain lashing at my face, ropes cutting into my palms.*

*Where did that black cloud come from? Oh no; this can't be happening. A rumble of thunder, and then...*

*Slash, a rip appears in the sail. I scream. How did that happen? I yell out to Jed.*

*I...I don't know. I never saw nothin' like it in my life.*

*Rip: there goes another one...and another.*

*Oh Jed! It's just as if...as if someone were slashing them with a cutlass!*

*It's Quaid, he says. It's his spirit...oh my god. He's taking his revenge...*

*And now we're veering way off course, due south-east, right towards the–*

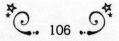

*Boom.*

*Towards the reef.*

'Nooo!'

This time I woke everyone up.

'What is it, *pethaki-mou*?' said Maro.

*The ship's sinking*, I nearly said. It had felt so real…

'I had a bad dream,' I said at last.

'Oh, sweetie!' Maro clambered out of her cubbyhole and down the ladder. 'What was it about?'

'Oh, it was just…I dreamed I was on a boat and it hit these rocks, and…anyway, I'm OK now, Maro, really; it's just a dumb dream.'

'You sure, baby?'

'Yeah, really…everyone, go back to sleep, I'm fine.'

And by now I was fine, actually – and my brain was buzzing over this latest development. What if *Quaid* was the key to the whole thing? Was *that* what this last dream was telling me? Beth had watched as the sail got slashed: 'How did that happen?' she'd asked. And Jed: 'I never saw nothin' like it in my life.' And the black cloud that came out of nowhere… What if Quaid did all that, for revenge? Was that even possible?

Honestly, the more I learned about ghosts, the more confusing it all got as to what they could and

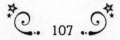

couldn't do. I decided there just had to be different *grades* of ghost.

'You sure you're OK?' whispered Flossie, as I scrabbled around on the ledge next to me for a pad of paper or something.

I badly wanted to tell her all about it, but I couldn't, not now. 'Yeah,' I whispered back. 'I just need to… You get to sleep, yeah? We'll talk in the morning.'

'OK,' said Flossie, turning over. 'G'night.'

Meanwhile I scrawled out some notes. After lots of crossings-out and corrections, I ended up with this:

Kitty Slade's Ghost Classification

Class E: Appear only to people with phantorama. Fade in and out, don't do much, can't communicate.

Class D: More active, can appear and speak to people with phantorama, but can't hear them.

Class C: Appear to and communicate with people with phantorama, both ways.

Class B: Covers anyone of levels C-E, but also appearing to people without phantorama. (Note: unproven as yet!)

Class A: Can do all of the above, plus

*actually move things/affect weather systems/do damage.*

'OK, conference,' I announced, after Maro had gone over to the house next morning.

Sam and Floss joined me on my bed, and I filled them in on the real details of my latest dream. I yawned. 'God, it took me *ages* to get to sleep after that!'

'So the ship *did* go down with the treasure!' said Sam. 'Imagine: those diamonds and pearls must still be out there somewhere!'

'Well of course, yes, amazing...but it's *Quaid* that I'm really excited about,' I said. 'Do you have any idea just what a powerful spirit he must be?'

'Pretty strong, all right,' said Sam.

I pulled out my ghost classification list. 'OK, this might seem very nerdy and un-Kittyish, but I've realised there are so many grades of power among ghosts, and I've come up with a list. Check it out.'

Sam and Flossie looked at it between them. 'So Captain Quaid's a Class A ghost,' said Sam.

'Exactly. I mean, look what he did: he sank the *Venus*!'

'Hang on,' said Flossie. 'You can't be saying he actually caused the storm?'

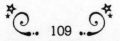

'Maybe. I'm not sure it would be possible for any ghost to *cause* a storm,' I said. 'But yeah, maybe he made it stronger, more violent. I felt that. And it was his spirit that ripped those sails, for sure.'

'How do you know?' asked Sam. 'Couldn't they have been ripped by the wind?'

'No. No way. You didn't see it. I'm telling you, there was a supernatural force at work – and Beth and Jed both knew it. They knew it was the spirit of Quaid, taking his revenge. But more than that: Beth's Class A, too – I saw her whip up the waves around her.'

'Oh yeah, I remember you saying,' said Flossie.

'So you know what I'm thinking?' I said. 'Quaid was avenging his death, OK – but it's more than that. He couldn't stand the thought of Beth and Jed making off with "his" jewels. I think he sank the ship because he felt that if he couldn't have that treasure, nobody should. And what do people do when they want something for themselves, and nobody else?'

'Lock it up,' said Flossie.

'OK, but suppose you couldn't lock it up.'

'Get a guard dog,' said Sam, half joking.

'Exactly!' I said. 'You *guard* it. Look, it's clear that Quaid felt *really strongly* about this. So maybe his ghost is still guarding the treasure, even now. That's why no one's found the wreck.'

'Really?' said Flossie. 'What, you think he's been sitting at the bottom of the sea for all these years?'

'It's possible!' I said. 'I mean look: we know ghosts can go underwater, because I've seen them, right? And there's no limit to how long they can stay there, because they don't need to breathe.'

'Very clever,' said Sam. 'I think it's a really interesting theory. But I'm just wondering...' He studied my list of ghost types. ' "Class A: can move things/affect weather systems/do damage"... D'you think you might have left something out?'

'Like what?'

'Like causing apparitions.'

'What? Oh, you mean the sightings of the *Venus*?'

'Exactly.'

'Right – I see what you mean! Maybe he's another grade above Beth, then. God, I mean, he must be! Look: those visions are hypnotising people into falling off cliffs, for heaven's sake! How's that happening? *Why* is it happening? We still don't know. But I'll tell you one thing: I know how close I came to going over the edge, and it is *real*.' I was shaking now. 'And if it's not Quaid who's causing that, then who?'

Sam and Floss looked at each other and shrugged.

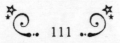

I sighed. 'Look, Quaid is the key to all of this, I swear. Here's another thing: Beth's trawling the mortal world, searching for her Jed, but why? I've been thinking about this, and it doesn't make sense that they're apart – until you think about Quaid. He's keeping her here. How, I don't know. And it's totally dumb, because if he thought it would get him Beth, well it hasn't worked, has it? Stupid! Powerful, but stupid.'

'Well, I suppose at least he's getting his own back,' said Sam. 'Making Beth miserable from being eternally separated from her beloved.'

'Oh, did I mention evil? Yes, that too. Stupid *and* evil. Man, I wish I could figure this out! I so want to stop him!'

We sat in silence, thinking. All those images from the dream filled my head: the lashing rain, the creaking masts, the churning waters, the huge waves…

*Weather systems.*

'Oh my god,' I said, snapping the notebook shut. 'I've just thought of something else!'

'What?'

'Something Bill said when I was talking to him the other day. He's an ex-fisherman, right? We were talking about shipwrecks, and he mentioned something about "no-go zones": danger spots at sea that the fishermen just don't ever go near. Well, it's just occurred to me:

what if *Captain Quaid's ghost* could create a disturbance like that in the waters?'

'Oh, to stop boats getting near the treasure?' said Flossie.

'Yes! It makes sense, doesn't it?'

'Hang on,' said Sam. 'I'm sure *fishermen* have all sorts of superstitions, but what about everyone else? I don't remember Uncle Sean talking about "no-go zones" – or our scuba instructor, for that matter.'

'OK, but maybe they don't know about this. Look, I just think it's worth considering, Sam. I really do!'

# Smugglers' Cove

The more I thought about Quaid, the more I hated him.

This was personal. He'd tried to kill me! I was convinced of it now. But I needed to find out how, why…I needed to explore it from every angle. And I needed Ashley's help.

'So, Ashley, what time are we going to the smuggler's cove?'

'Oh, that…well…'

'Ashley! You promised! And now I've had another dream: I'm *this* close to figuring this all out, I swear. Plus, the longer we ignore the situation with Megan–'

'Yes, well, sorry, but I don't actually know how to get there,' said Ashley, averting her eyes.

'Ooh, you *so* do!' I said, grabbing her arm. 'Look, *please*. C'mon, we've been over this. I need to get to the bottom of this whole *Venus* thing, you know that. Even

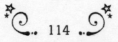

if you couldn't care less about Megan, think of that. You're the one who told me about those people who died after seeing it. You know about my phantorama, you know that I might have the power to put a stop to this… Ashley, someone could die very soon! It's been happening every thirty years, and the last one was thirty years ago. It could have been me!'

'OK, OK!' said Ashley. 'But it'll have to wait till tomorrow. Today's completely crammed: I've got English coursework to do, and stacks of homework…'

I sighed. 'All right, all right…but no more excuses, OK? We do this tomorrow, definitely.'

Ashley rolled her eyes. 'Yes, I promise.'

Meanwhile, Sam and I worked on finding out anything else we could. After my last experience at the Lobster Pot I was kind of scared to go there again, but it had one major thing going for it: free wi-fi. So we took the laptop and had some ve-e-ery slow hot chocolates while we got stuck into the internet. There was absolutely nothing about Beth Trewin or Jed Lannion. There was some stuff about the *Venus*, but nothing we didn't know already…Zachary Quaid, though; we got some stuff on him.

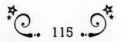

Zachary Quaid, 1668-1728: notorious privateer, modelled himself on his infamous predecessor, Captain James Morgan.

'OK, finally!' I said. 'Only the date of his death could be wrong, of course.'

There were some details about where he went, on which boats, what he brought back. There had been some really successful raids before his final outing to Spain with the *Venus*. 'Looks like he'd made himself pretty rich already,' I said. 'He was a pirate, near enough, wasn't he?'

'And so was your friend Beth Trewin,' said Sam.

'Well…yeah, I guess.' I glanced around; I kept expecting to see her hunched in a corner somewhere, ready to play another fishy trick on me. In a way I was dreading it, but at the same time I really wanted to see her again, because of course I had a gazillion questions to ask her. But I guess she was busy just being in my head – for now, at least. I wondered if I'd ever see her again – and if I would be able to handle it.

I studied my notes, as I drained the last of the chocolate in my cup. 'OK, something's missing,' I said. 'Those no-go zones – we need to find out more about them.' I did a search on 'fisherman's no-go areas', but all I got was some stuff about some other kinds of no-go

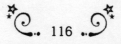

zones, nothing to do with fishing boats, and some other stuff about fish conservation.

'I think you're going to have to go back and talk to your man Bill,' said Sam.

I sighed. 'Yeah, I guess you're right. Ha! *How* am I going to ask him about this?'

Well, I figured it out, and managed to drag Ashley away from her schoolwork just long enough to come with me to Bill's place. As usual, he was pottering around in his garden, doing god-knows-what.

'Hello there!' he said. 'Here, you've not seen our Megan, have yer? Only she's not been around for a day or so.'

'Really?' said Ashley.

We looked at each other. A *day* or so? I wondered whether he'd seen her since we had yesterday. I didn't know whether to mention that or not. Not, I decided.

'Have you told the police?' Ashley asked him.

'Oh, no, no!' Bill waved his hand. 'She's probably just stoppin' out wi' friends, like she's a mind to now an' then. She said to me 'erself, she said, "Pop, if I's a bit absent for awhile, you're not to go worrying, or calling on the law; I'll be awright. Jus' bide your time, an' I'll be back afore long, an' I'll bring you somethin' nice, an' all.'

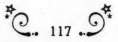

We exchanged glances again. '*Does* she bring you something nice?' I asked.

Bill's eye suddenly averted. 'Oh, well, you know: jus' a nice bit o' baccy or somethin', to let her dad know she loves 'im! Never you mind; I'm not worried or anythin', just wondered if you'd happened to cross paths.'

He did seem amazingly cheerful, considering; I guess he was used to it. 'Well, we'll keep an eye out for her,' I said. 'Erm, Bill, I had a question…for my project?'

'Oh, yeah?'

'Yes, well…you mentioned something about "no-go zones", out at sea?'

'That's right, uh-huh.'

'Well, I was wondering…are any of those, like, right around here, close to Pelporth?'

'Oh sure,' said Bill. 'Goin' west of here always was a bloomin' nuisance, what with havin' to steer clear o' that one. Oh, you can call on the help of the saints an' all, help calm things down, but only so much you can do. Best to go *round*, y'know? Good hauls to be had, though, once yer do. I remember one time…'

He rambled on for a bit with some boring fishing story; we listened politely. Then, when he paused, I jumped in quickly: 'You wouldn't happen to have the coordinates, would you?'

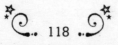

Bill frowned. 'Eh?'

'The coordinates... It's for my project.'

'Oh! You're not plannin' to test it out, I hope!'

'No, no.'

'Good. 'Cause you don't want to be doing that, I'm tellin' yer. Well...come in for a minute.'

We followed him into the dark cottage, which was full of clutter and smelled of tobacco and mould. 'Let me see now,' he said, rubbing his hand over his sparse silver-haired head. He went to a pile of books and stuff on the floor beside a worn-out armchair, and picked out a folded dog-eared map. He opened it up – it was practically falling apart – then pointed to a spot in the sea near Pelporth, which was marked by a big 'X' in red biro. 'There.' He handed the map to me. 'Here, take it.'

'Thanks.'

'No, I mean, you can have it. I've no use for it no more.'

'Really? Wow, thanks!'

'Don't mention it,' said Bill. 'There ye go, now.'

'Bye, Bill,' said Ashley. 'If we see Megan, we'll remind her to come see you.'

Bill nodded. 'You do that. Cheerio!'

'There's one thing you need to know about the

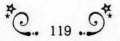

smugglers' cove,' said Ashley on Sunday morning. 'Well, a couple of things, actually. But the main thing is, most of the time it's flooded.'

'Oh! How come?'

'There's just not much to it; the beach is really narrow at the best of times. There's only about two hours in the day when it's safe to go there at all. And once we're there, we can't stay too long. I checked the timing of the tides: we have to leave here no later than say, one o'clock.'

'So I guess that means that if Megan was planning to go there today, she'd have to go at that time too,' said Sam.

'Uh, yeah…' said Ashley, looking away. Obviously still having *issues* where Megan was concerned.

'OK, well the upside, then, is that it's easier to catch her,' I said. Ashley studied her fingernails. 'Because we wouldn't want something terrible to happen to her, *would* we, Ashley,' I added pointedly. 'Not if there was something we could do to prevent it.'

Ashley cleared her throat. 'Yeah, well, the *downside* is, you stick around too long, you drown. Not even an Olympic world champion swimmer can fight that surf, with all those rocks about. So let's *really* keep a close eye on the time: we have to be out of there by 2.45.'

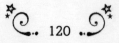

'OK.'

We had it all planned perfectly…and then we got delayed.

'When are they ever going to leave?' I hissed to Ashley. Ty had gone out some time ago, but we were still waiting on Maro, Sean and Phoebe, who was just now taking yet *another* phone call.

'I don't know! Should've left an hour ago.'

'Look, why don't we just go anyway?' I suggested.

'But there's all that work Maro's set you…'

'We can do it later! She should have set it yesterday, when *you* were busy; it's *so* annoying.'

'I dunno… We might have to put this off for another day…'

'No! There's still time, right? Let's not give up yet.'

We all sighed with relief as Phoebe finally ended the call, and she and Maro headed out.

'Bye, kids!' Maro yelled from the front door. 'Be good!'

'Yeah,' we called back. 'Bye!'

Phoebe's car coughed into life, and they drove off. Three minutes later, we were off on our way to the smugglers' cove.

'OK, I think we've got just enough time,' said Ashley. 'If we move fast.'

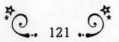

We moved fast. 'So what else do we need to know about this place?' I asked.

'Huh?'

'You said there was the tide…and something else.'

'Oh yeah, right. Well, I've only been there once, but I do remember it being kind of smeechy.'

'Kind of *what*?'

'It *stinks*. One reason no one really goes there – even the ones who've figured out how. Plus you have to go through this narrow cave to get to it, which is scary as hell.'

She wasn't kidding.

The cave was at the far end of Bosreath Cove, where I'd first connected with Beth. It was just a great long crack in the rock, hidden behind another outcrop of rocks; it was easy to see how I hadn't noticed it last time. I half expected to see Beth there again. But…same as at the Lobster Pot, no sign of her. She'd set her challenge, and there was nothing else to discuss as far as she was concerned.

'I'm warning you, it's not for claustrophobics,' said Ashley, as we approached the entrance to the cave. 'Are you ready?'

We stepped in, and flicked on our torches. The beams of light made horror chamber sculptures out of the craggy, sloping walls. Up, up, up the walls rose above our heads, never quite touching. I felt the cold, clammy air penetrate my bones. Underneath our feet, the gravel crunched loud as a giant's footsteps. Ahead all I could see was Sam's back; that's how narrow it was. Beyond him was blackness, barely lifted by torchlight; I kept glancing back for those reassuring glimpses of daylight. Then that hole closed up too.

'H-how far is it to the other side?' asked Flossie.

'Erm…I'm not sure,' Ashley called back from the head of the line. The cave made her voice sound metallic.

'Don't you remember?'

'No,' said Ashley. 'See, last time I…well, I sort of didn't go all the way through.'

'You what?' Flossie's voice was several octaves higher. 'Oh, *great.*'

'But you said—' I began.

'Well, you were pressuring me!' said Ashley. 'Anyway, it does open up the other side, I promise.'

'Don't worry about it, Floss,' said Sam. 'We'll be OK.'

'All right, well, let's just get there as soon as possible, please,' I said. My throat felt like it had a gobstopper stuck in it, and my breathing had gone all shallow.

We trudged on, not saying a word. *Crunch, crunch, crunch.*

Then the air changed.

'Eurgh!' said Flossie. 'What is that *smell*?'

'I told you it was smeechy,' said Ashley. 'That's good: it's a sign we're getting to the other side.'

I thought I could make out the distant sound of waves. Soon there was another noise, too: a high-pitched buzzing sound. Flies.

*Crunch, crunch, crunch.*

Now the smell grew stronger. 'Urgh!' I gasped. 'That is *rank*.'

'It's only seaweed,' said Ashley. 'But...argh; there's *lots* of flies here, watch out. The good news is, I see daylight.'

'Oh...great.' I didn't mean to sound sarcastic; I *was* actually relieved. But now the reeking seaweed was about on a level with a fishmonger's bin on a hot day during a bin-men's strike – with about as many flies, too. As we emerged from the tunnel, we all swatted wildly at the great cloud of flies, while practically gagging from the bad smell.

'Gah! How can *seaweed* reek so much?' I asked, attempting to hold my nose while still fighting off the flies. 'Are you sure that's all it is?'

'Sometimes it's like that,' said Ashley.

Now we were out in the open. The beach was

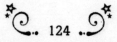

almost completely covered with black, bubbly seaweed. The cliff-face loomed over it, a gigantic sideways-leaning wall. Ahead, huge jagged rocks jutted up from the ground, like a pile of giant's gravestones that had toppled against one another.

And the stench. And the flies.

'God, no wonder no one ever comes here!' said Sam.

'Oh, they do,' said Ashley, pointing. 'Look.'

Beer cans and cigarette butts decorated the seaweed. I remembered what Oliver said about his brother coming here for a party. 'It can't always be this gross, then,' I said, slapping away at the flies.

'Let's see what's beyond those rocks,' said Ashley, pointing to the gravestoney-things.

Drawing nearer, we found a gap between the gigantic slabs, just wide enough to squeeze through. No more pebbles here: now we walked across smooth, flattish rocks. Ahead was another cliff-face with a massive black hole in the middle. Another cave.

Suddenly, Ashley grabbed hold of my sleeve and yanked me down behind a large rock. '*Psst!* Get down!' she told the others. 'I saw something.'

We huddled behind the rock.

A loud whistle pierced the air, making us jump. It came from somewhere near the big cave.

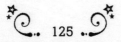

'There's someone there!' I hissed.

We huddled in silence. After a moment, there was another whistle: *pi-peeeyit!*

'Sounds like a signal,' whispered Sam. 'Maybe they're expecting someone.'

It seemed this person was waiting on a reply – which probably meant they'd heard something. In other words, they'd heard *us* – there was no one else around. I didn't dare whisper back to Sam. Instead, I took my phone and tapped out a text message:

## No whispering from now on

I showed it to the others; they all nodded. Even with all the noise from the sea and the wind, we couldn't risk making a sound. We had *no idea* who was waiting in that cave – and we weren't about to find out. I was dying to see if it was Megan, but it was way too risky to take a peek.

We waited.

The flies were driving us quietly crazy; we twitched like lunatics. Perhaps whoever was in the cave would give up and leave. I deleted the message on my phone – and noticed the time. Already ten past two! I nudged Ashley and pointed; she raised her eyebrows, nodded, then shrugged. What could we do? We were stuck here until either something happened, or two forty-five, whichever came first.

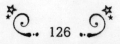

I shifted position; my right leg was going to sleep. I thought about Megan. For all we knew, she'd already been and gone – she'd had a whole hour to do that.

Still we waited. Nobody came. At least by now we could be pretty sure that whoever was in the cave hadn't seen us. Flossie busied herself with making tiny plaits in her hair; she began humming as she did so. I put my hand over her mouth. She hung her head exaggeratedly, signalling 'bored'.

We waited some more. By now I didn't even notice the smell. The sun came out; warmed by it, I felt myself drift off...

*Pi-peeeyit!*

Another whistle. I jolted upright.

It came from a different direction. Then, a moment later, a response from inside the cave. We huddled tightly together behind the rocks. And then there she was: Megan. Walking towards the cave, carrying a backpack.

We couldn't see inside the cave. But we needed to get closer if we were going to hear anything. I tapped Sam and Floss on the shoulder, and jerked my head in that direction; we crept closer, grateful for the lack of gravel in this part of the cove, and the noise of the waves.

We listened. At first, we heard nothing. Suddenly I felt uncomfortable; maybe Megan was secretly meeting

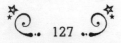

some boyfriend? But after a moment, we heard her say: 'It's all there: fifty grand.'

'Yeah, yeah…just wait, awright? I'm nearly done,' came a man's voice.

'Yeah, it's just I got to–'

'*Tss!* Shut it!'

'The *tide*, Howie,' said Megan. 'I'm a bit late.'

The tide! It would be coming in at two forty-five. I checked the time: it was two thirty-seven.

# Diamond-shaped Idea

'Howie' didn't seem to care about the tide; I could only think he must've had a boat moored up inside the cave or something. 'Well, you shoulda thought of that, shouldn't you!' he snapped at Megan.

'Yeah, but my dad–'

'I'm NEARLY DONE, OK? Go on; you know where the stuff is. Fill 'er up.'

Shuffling sounds as Megan moved around, and 'filled her up'.

Meanwhile, I was making calculations in my head. The man was counting money, I guessed. Probably wasn't going to let Megan go until he'd finished. And it was a lot: just one 'grand', I knew from the cop shows, was a thousand pounds – and Megan had brought fifty times that. There were just ten minutes to go before we'd have to leave – which meant we couldn't wait for

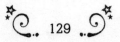

Megan to leave, because that would mean having to give her plenty of time to get ahead of us if we didn't want to get caught – time we didn't have.

I nudged Ashley, pointed to the time, and jerked my thumb in the direction of 'away'.

Her eyes widened; she nodded vigorously.

We turned and left. We got past the tombstone rocks, and there, with all the spectacular bad timing of a particularly bonkers ghost, stood Beth Trewin. Staring at me, hands on hips.

'Oh!' I gasped.

Ashley was already ahead of me. She turned and frowned. 'Huh?'

'It's, um, Beth.'

The thing about ghosts is, their appearance never changes – at least, they're always in the same clothes. And here she was, in that same red headscarf, same crumpled shirt and jacket, same dirt. Same clenched right fist. What had changed was her expression, which looked thundery enough to bring on a storm.

'What use are thee, eh?' she snarled, blocking my way. 'Ye meddle in my affairs, say ee'm going to help an' all, but 'tis all lies!'

'No, no!' I said in a loud whisper. 'Look, I promise–'

'Shh!' hissed Sam, coming up alongside me. 'They'll

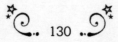

hear you! C'mon!' He grabbed my arm and pulled.

'Look, this is kind of a bad time,' I told Beth, then gasped as a wave whooshed up and completely covered my feet. 'Aah! I got to go!' I cried, then dived after the others. But the backdraught of the wave pulled seaweed with it, entangling my feet; I tripped and fell, twisting my ankle and landing face down in the stinking mass.

'Lies! Lies!' yelled Beth.

Ashley rushed over. 'Kitty! Are you all right?'

I pulled myself into a sitting position, and another wave swept up. Great; soaked again. Sam lifted me up and my ankle twinged painfully. 'Ow, ow!' I mouthed silently.

'Quick!' said Flossie. 'There's someone coming!'

'Aaah!' I couldn't help crying, as I limped on towards the cave entrance. We all piled into the pitch black space. Ashley and Sam fumbled around for their torches. I couldn't tell whether Beth was following me, and I wasn't going to try and find out.

'My torch isn't working!' hissed Sam. I heard him bashing it, but it didn't help.

'Oh no,' squeaked Flossie. 'Ashley, *please…*'

Then came the sound of whooshing water. Was that…could it be…?

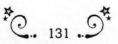

'There!' said Ashley, as at last her beam flickered on. Then, 'Oh god…watch out!'

A great surge of seawater came hurtling in behind us. It frothed and churned and bashed against our knees – and it was rising.

'We really have no time now,' said Ashley – kind of stating the obvious.

*OK, calm, calm*, I told myself – but I was anything but calm. All I could think of was that I'd seen the *Venus*, and I was doomed, doomed…it was time. The thirty years were up. I'd thought I'd had a lucky escape, but really…this was it.

Then the water sucked away; thank god! We squelched on as fast as we could.

'Who's there?' came a voice – Megan.

We didn't say anything; we just carried on, a little faster. My ankle was killing me. I could hear Megan's splashing footsteps following us; she was speeding up too. I could see the flashes of light from her torch bouncing on the walls.

Daylight appeared; we were getting close to Bosreath Cove. I was the last in the line; just as I got to the opening, Megan caught up with me and threw herself on top of me, pushing me to the ground.

*Oof!* I felt the air whoosh from my lungs as

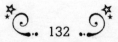

I was clobbered by the wet stones.

'Kitty!' cried Flossie.

'Get off her!' cried Sam, and now he was in the pile too.

Face down in the shingle, I could just see enough with my right eye to know there was another huge wave crashing towards us. Then the weight came off me, and I scrambled to my feet – only to be slammed sideways by the great hard salty wall of water.

'What are you playing at?' demanded Megan, as the wave washed back. Her voice floated thinly on the howling air.

'N-nothing!' I cried feebly. I got to my feet, soaked to the skin; still Megan clung like a limpet to my sleeve.

'You!' she yelled, spotting Ashley. 'What the hell are you doing here?'

Ashley looked almost green. 'Megan, the tide–'

A seagull screamed overhead. I turned and saw what Ashley saw: a massive wave, heading towards us.

We all just ran. When we got to the other side of the bay, we scrambled up the rocks and scrub till we got well above the high-tide line. Then Megan, who was ahead of us all, stood up and turned.

'OK,' she gasped, red-faced and dripping. 'What will it take to shut you up?'

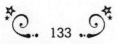

'What will it *take*?' said Ashley.

Megan's face was hard and mean; she was shivering as she slung the backpack off her shoulder. She undid it and reached inside. 'Yeah. What do you want? Gold earrings? Rolex watch? Here.' She held out a plastic ziplock bag with something glinting gold inside.

'Where did that come from?' asked Ashley.

'No questions,' said Megan. 'Here.' She grabbed Ashley's wrist and forced the object into her hand, closing the fingers around it. She turned to us. 'You too…here—'

'No, no!' cried Ashley. 'You don't understand! We don't want your bribes. We just…we were worried about you. And so is your dad, by the way.'

'Yeah, you need to go and see him,' I added.

Megan ignored this; she was still staring at Ashley, her face scrunched up in disbelief. 'You, worried about me?' She let out a dry, hard laugh. 'Oh, right. Like *you* care!'

'I do!' protested Ashley weakly.

'Ha!' snapped Megan. 'Don't make me laugh. You blank me every time, like you never knew me. You're a *snob*, that's what you are!'

Ashley's jaw hung open. '*Snob?* Are you surprised I don't talk to you? Don't you *remember* how you used to go around telling everyone I was "terminally uncool"?'

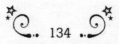

Megan's mouth was twisted. 'Right, and in all these years, you've never worked that one out, eh?' Her chin was wobbling now. 'For god's sake, can't you see, I was *jealous*. I've never been any good at anything like you are. And you had the nice house, the holidays abroad, and...and...I wanted a voice like yours! What I wouldn't have given for a talent like that...*any* talent, really...' Her eyes were glassy. 'Oh, forget it,' she went on. 'You'll never understand in a million years. You've no idea what it's like to have to scrounge pennies for a bacon sandwich...to freeze in winter, 'cause you can't afford the fuel. So you just mind your own business, and I'll mind mine, OK?'

'No!' I said, stepping forward. 'We can't do that; not now.'

'Oh, another little Miss Superior, eh? Here, I've seen you around, ain't I? Nosy parker, ain'tcha? Can't *wait* to get the bad girl into trouble, eh? See her get–'

'Whoah, whoah. What do you mean, *get* you into trouble?' Sam interrupted. 'I think you're already in trouble, aren't you?'

'Yes,' I added, 'and anyway, who said we were going to tell on you?'

Megan looked surprised. 'You're not?'

'No,' said Ashley. 'But you've got to report that Howie guy, and whoever else is involved in this.'

'Report them?' snapped Megan. 'Are you out of your flippin' mind? They'd kill me!'

'They couldn't kill you if they were in prison,' Flossie pointed out.

'Of course they could!' said Megan. 'It's a whole network. Oh, and you can forget about anonymous tip-offs an' all…that wouldn't work. They'd know it was me.' She shook her head slowly. 'Ha! You kids…you got no idea. Anyway I don't *want* to report them, and you can't make me.'

'Really?' I said. 'Well…but what if you didn't need them?' I just sort of blurted this out, before the idea was fully formed in my head.

Megan squinted at me. 'Didn't *need* them? What do you mean?'

'I mean…'

The idea came together now – a diamond-shaped idea. Suppose Bill really had supplied the vital clue to the location of the wreck of the *Venus*, and its precious cargo? There would be a reward for that, wouldn't there? OK, I was bluffing here, but anything that made Megan think again about her situation had to be worth it:

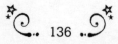

'I *mean*,' I repeated, 'what if I knew of a way that your dad – and you too – could come into quite a lot of money, very soon, and you could wave goodbye to all this. What would you say then?'

# Rescue Mission

'What on earth happened to you?' asked Phoebe.

Well, we did look a bit of a state, in our very soggy clothes. Plus we were all out of breath from our dash back, trying to beat the others to the house so we could change before they saw us.

'Sorry, Mum,' said Ashley.

'I thought you were–'

'Yes, I know I said we were going to stay here, but the thing is… Look, we know someone who's in trouble. I can't say who it is or anything, but…Dad?'

Sean was sitting at the kitchen table, where – unusually for him – he was chilling out with a cup of tea and the Sunday papers. 'What's up, Ashley? What's happened?'

Maro emerged from the next room; I think she'd been napping on the sofa, judging by the crease down

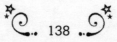

her cheek. 'What's going on? Oh, *pethakia*, look at you!'

'It's OK, Maro, we're fine,' I said. 'It's just…we saw something just now.'

'Ark!' cried Winston the cockatoo, joining in with the general hubbub and flapping around like a panicked parent.

Phoebe, Sean and Maro all spoke at the same time:

'What?'

'What did you see?'

'Who's in trouble?'

Phoebe already had the phone in her hand. Ashley rushed at her. 'No – please don't call the police.'

'Ashley, if someone's–' Phoebe started.

'No, listen, we have a plan,' said Ashley. 'It's all going to work out fine…well, that is, if you'll do something for us, Dad.'

'Me? What can I do?'

'Can you take us out in the boat?' said Ashley. 'Like, now?'

'Now? Does someone need rescuing? Because if they do, then it's the lifeboat people you–'

'No, no, it's nothing like that,' said Ashley.

'Ashley, for heaven's sake, will you just tell us what happened!' said Phoebe. 'You can't expect your dad to

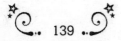

take the boat out at a moment's notice – especially when he's having his first day off in ages.'

'Anyway, it's late!' added Maro. 'It's gone three-thirty. Now go and put some dry things on–'

'Oh, *please*, Dad!' said Ashley.

'Your mum's right, Ashley,' said Sean. 'We need to know who's in trouble, and why.'

'Ark!' went Winston, as if agreeing with him.

'You will!' insisted Ashley. 'But *afterwards*. It's…it's Kitty's idea.'

All the adults looked at me. I took a deep breath. 'All right, look,' I said. 'This may seem mad, but trust me, it'll all make sense eventually.'

I could tell they weren't impressed. Phoebe was still *this* close to calling the police, while Maro was hovering, ready to chip in with her own OTT nonsense. Sean just sat there looking like the last thing in the world he wanted to do was move.

I thought about the *Venus*, and the bad omen. I was tempted to yell out, 'This is your chance to save lives!' but I knew they would think I was completely hysterical. The cold from the wet clothes was starting to get to me, and I was shivering. I put on my best, rational, grown-up-sounding voice, and said as calmly as I could, 'We just want to get this person out of trouble. And…I've got

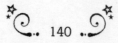

some information. About the whereabouts of something. At the bottom of the sea.'

Maro looked at Phoebe. Phoebe looked at Sean. Sean and Phoebe looked at Maro.

Winston squawked.

'Go, Sean,' said Phoebe suddenly. 'Do it.' She widened her eyes at Sean in a way that hinted at a lot of words that weren't being said. I couldn't help wondering *what* words. Was there something she knew, but wasn't letting on about? Like…my phantorama? Well, if she knew about that, then she would have some idea as to where I'd got my information from, and why I felt I couldn't say more…

We all looked at Sean.

'Well, you're right, it does seem mad,' he said. 'And how do you plan to find this spot, anyway?'

'I can show you.' I went into the hall and got Bill's map from the jacket I'd worn yesterday. I opened it up and showed Sean the spot marked in red biro. 'Here.'

He studied the fragile old map, cleared his throat. 'OK. Since these are…*special* circumstances…let's give it a go. But first of all, let us be absolutely clear about one thing. This person who's "in trouble": there's no chance that any delay caused by our doing this is going to make their situation worse, I hope?'

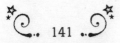

'It's not going to make any difference,' said Ashley.

Sean sighed deeply. 'Right. I'll talk to Ty.'

Phoebe put her arms around his shoulders. 'OK, great. Now *please* go and get into some dry things, guys, before you freeze to death.'

Just as we were leaving, I noticed her lean down and whisper something in Sean's ear.

I followed Ashley into her room. 'OK, what does Phoebe know about what's going on?'

'Nothing!' said Ashley, while busying herself with finding some things to change into. *Really* busying herself. As in, the avoiding eye contact kind of busying herself.

'You told her, didn't you,' I said. 'About my phantorama.'

'No, I didn't,' said Ashley, inspecting a sweater she'd pulled from a drawer.

I folded my arms at her. 'Oh, you *so* did!'

Then she looked me straight in the eye. 'You know what? I didn't have to – she already knew.'

This threw me a bit. 'She did?'

'Yeah, Maro told her. Dad knows too. They've just not mentioned it around you, because Maro told them you're kind of sensitive about it. It's why they didn't tell me. They figured you'd talk about it if you wanted to.'

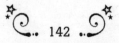

'What…so Maro told them, but didn't tell *me* she'd told them. Huh!'

'Well, she was hardly going to do that, was she?' said Ashley. 'Or what would be the point of making them keep quiet about it?'

'But she said she'd tell your mum *one day*! I sort of thought…I dunno, I thought that meant not for ages yet. And I kind of thought she'd consult me first.'

'Come on, Kitty, you can't really blame her. Your *mum* had it – have you forgotten that? My mum's sister! My mum grew up with all the weirdness of…sorry, I mean–'

'It's OK, I know what you mean.'

'Plus, she knew it was hereditary. I can see why it would've been hard for Maro not to say anything.'

'OK…OK…it's all right, I get it now. You know, it's easy for me to forget about all that, 'cause I never really knew my mum…' I felt a lump rise in my throat.

'I know,' said Ashley. She gave me a hug – which made it worse, of course. I stood there for a minute, all lumpy and teary, then I pulled myself together.

'By the way,' Ashley added, 'I never said anything about you seeing the *Venus* or anything.'

'OK, good,' I said. 'But I guess your mum's worked out that I've got some important information from

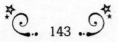

a ghost – not *strictly* true – and that's why she's given this the go-ahead.'

'Exactly. You see? It's a good thing that they know. Ooh, Kit, I'm so excited now, I can hardly breathe!'

# Gruesome Guards

The boat clipped along happily for a while. Everyone had come this time – even Maro and Phoebe. This was all much too intriguing for them to miss out on. I was ready; sitting with Sam and Ty in my second-hand diving suit, I truly felt like someone on a mission.

Well, actually, I was nervous as hell. For one thing, I was a bit scared of what I might find down there that was capable of causing so much disturbance in the water. This could be dangerous. It also bothered me that we might not find anything at all. What if the water was too deep for me to dive there? I could only go down eighteen metres – not very far at all. And then if we didn't find anything, what would we do about Megan? We'd just have to report her – and I *so* did not want to do that!

I was busy bouncing back and forth between these

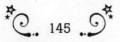

two worries, when I remembered something else: I hadn't actually warned Sean about this being one of Bill's 'no-go zones'. I realised this a bit too late – after the boat had started to rock.

'Oh *Kitta na thiss*! It's getting rough out here,' said Maro, clutching her seat tightly.

'Yes, it is rather,' said Sean. 'Strange! Bit sudden. Still, we're nearly there.'

The turbulence soon got worse, jerking us this way and that, making us lurch into one another.

Poor Maro was turning green. 'How long is this going to take?'

Sean grimaced. 'Erm…well, hard to tell…*whoops!* Water sprayed over the side; Maro and Phoebe leaped out of the way.

'Oh, this was a bad idea, bad idea!' cried Maro.

'I'm sorry!' I cried.

'Kit, are you sure about this?' said Sam. He was looking a bit green, too.

Then Ty called out, 'Look, Dad! See over there? It's much calmer.'

'You're right,' said Sean, gazing out in the direction Ty was pointing. 'That is…that's bizarre. How can it be so calm like that, in the midst of all this? I never saw anything like it.'

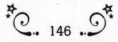

'Why don't you drop anchor over where it's calm, then we can dive from there,' suggested Ty.

'Oh, yes please,' said Maro.

'All right,' said Sean. 'But bear with me; got a bit more roughness to go through before we get there. *Very* strange...'

'I'm *so* sorry, Maro,' I said.

Maro waved a hand. 'Oh, it's not your fault, *Kitaki-mou.*'

*Oh yes it is*, I felt like saying – but I didn't.

We all sat grim-faced as we got through the next few lurching and rolling minutes. Then, as quickly as it had started, the turbulence calmed down, and we were puttering along happily again. Finally, Sean and Ty spent some time figuring out the best spot to anchor the boat, well clear of the rough waters.

At last it was time to go down. Sean checked his surveying equipment, and told us that back where we would be heading underwater, there was a ridge. 'It's quite a bit shallower there,' he said. 'Only about twenty-two, twenty-three metres.'

'All right! Cool,' I said – trying to *seem* cool about the whole thing, when really I was a quivering jelly. Twenty-three metres was deeper than I could go – but that needn't matter. With any luck, it might just be shallow

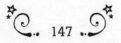

enough for me to see the sea bed. All depended how clear the waters were.

But it turned out I needn't have worried about that. 'Here, you'll need these,' said Ty, reaching into a storage trunk and pulling out some torches. 'They strap to your wrist – see?'

'OK, thanks.'

'OK,' said Ty, picking up his underwater film camera. 'In we go. Must say, I'm dying of curiosity now!'

'So are we all,' said Phoebe.

'*Kali epitychia!*' said Maro. 'Good luck! Come back alive!'

Diving was like entering another world. Well, duh, because that's what it is, right? Spacey, floaty, dark world, full of bizarre creatures that could never exist in the dry world. And we couldn't see more than three or four metres in any direction; beyond was too murky. So that was pretty spooky, for starters.

And diving made me go inside my own head, in a way I never normally did. Even though I was with others – and of course I was *always* with others for safety – I felt more alone than ever, packed inside a neoprene casing and crazy Dr Who breathing equipment, hearing nothing but the occasional eerie pinging of water pressure in the rocks, and my own amplified breathing:

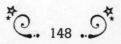

it felt like my own little planet. I couldn't talk to anyone. I could point, gesticulate, shake my head or nod – but that was about it. Actually, that hadn't really bothered me until now. But this time was different.

Boy, was it ever.

We went down. The water was deep here; at first we were just propelling ourselves with our giant frog-feet through sea-space. Then the ridge came into view below, just a little way ahead of us; a mass of angry alien weed. Here, with the help of our torches, we could see the sea bed. I watched a big crab scuttle under a rock; it perched there, just visible, spiny mouthparts working away. Crazy alien creature; whoever invented a mouth like that? A see-through prawn danced past my face, tiny organs pumping, like the ghost of a prawn.

Then, *whoosh!* Something thumped me sideways. I went into a somersault, not knowing which way was up, or what had just hit me. All I saw was a dark figure disappearing into the gloom. Then another shape emerged. A seal? It was large enough. But no…oh no, this was no seal.

This was something horrible.

It had a human face – but one that was very, very wrong. For one thing, it was upside-down. For another, it was all squished into an expression of complete terror.

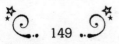

As the rest of the figure appeared, I saw that the face was upside-down because the body it was attached to was moving in a way no human body was ever meant to – much like the crab I'd just been watching, in fact. Back arched, belly up, cruelly distorted arms and legs supporting it.

If I could have cried out, I would have done.

Then another figure appeared in front of me; I jumped. But it was just Ty. Ty, who obviously couldn't see the crab-man, or he'd be in a whole different mental place right now, and his eyes would be showing it. But he could see that I was troubled; he waved to me, signalling, 'Are you all right?'

I hung there, paralysed. Finally I nodded, gave the thumbs up.

Meanwhile my head was exploding. OK, you knew there was something weird going on down here, I told myself. You were right! Congratulations; deal with it. Only…just what was I dealing with here?

*Thump.*

Again, I was knocked sideways; this time I saw it more clearly, the ragged figure of a man, ripped clothing trailing behind him as he hurtled past. He turned and grimaced at me. Actually, he couldn't do anything *but* grimace; his face was nearly all melted away. Just staring

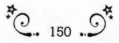

eyes, a hole where the nose should be, and skeletal, grinning teeth with no lips. Before I knew it, I was surrounded by bizarre figures: a woman who looked normal except that her head was on back-to-front. Another, in a big-skirted Victorian dress, was bent forward at right angles at the waist, then again at the neck, so that her face was turned upwards. A man in tweedy clothes with goggles on his head moved in the water as if he had no joints; everything just twisted any old way. Others, each in clothing of different decades, but every one mashed up and horrific.

All of them were closing in on me. Who were they?

I could hear my breathing in my ears like a steam engine. I felt as if I might throw up – but I couldn't. If I did, I'd choke. I was dimly aware of Sam and Ty nearby; they were OK, but they seemed to be having a hard time moving forward. The ghosts – they *were* ghosts, I was sure of that – were repelling them, just as effectively as they were me; the only difference was that Ty and Sam couldn't see them. Lucky for some.

The twisted, terrifying faces loomed closer…and now I began to understand. That woman with the back-to-front head; she was in modern dress, but something about the style of hair, the scarf she wore, the patterned sweater…could she be from the 1980s? And the man in

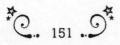

the tweeds and goggles…he did look sort of nineteen-twenties-ish…

Now it all began to slot into place in my head. Were these the other people who had seen the *Venus?* Harriet Jenkins, 1982; Norman Cavendish, 1957. David Bunhill, 1929…oh wow. And the rest of them, from further back in time, all here, now…

They were all here.

And they were gathered here for a purpose; to make it impossible for us to go any further. This was Quaid's doing – it had to be. These were his prisoners – doomed to lurk down here, protecting his hoard. Now I was so freaked out, I thought I would faint. I had to get back up to the surface. But no! I couldn't miss this chance – what might be my only chance to see if it was true; that this was the site of the wreck of the *Venus.*

And it had to be – didn't it? If I could just…

They closed in, encircling the three of us. The figures turned in a big circle, and now they were going faster, and faster, and faster…

The force of their movement was creating a whirlpool effect. I felt myself being pulled into it – saw the others being carried as well. Ty looked seriously alarmed. He pointed upwards, and indicated the pressure valve on his jacket…he was telling us we had to

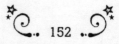

go back to the surface, and fast.

I nodded, but I wasn't ready to give up just yet. Because beyond the whirling ghosts, I was getting tantalising glimpses of something else...some*one* else. A bearded figure, lurking down below. I fought with all my might against the clamouring phantoms with their awful gargoyle faces, but my limbs moved like feathers through treacle.

But there was another glimpse! His face, looking up at us, laughing. It was the same face I'd seen in the dream; the same bulbous nose, the same ugly leer.

Captain Quaid.

# 16

# Missing Person

He was laughing.

Big, ugly Quaid, sitting there. I got a glimpse of him, and then *whoosh!* Gone, as I was carried along in the merry-go-round of horrible spectres. Then around again: ha ha ha! Perched there on the rocks like King Neptune himself, fat belly bulging over his lap. Thin tendrils of hair curling around his bulldog head. But what about the treasure? I couldn't see anything…but I wasn't going to give up now.

Then *whoosh*; off again. Round and round, faster and faster. I reached for my pressure valve and opened it up, releasing more air into my jacket to buoy me up. My fingers were fumbling; *careful.* I had to release just the right amount of air; too little, and I'd be sucked down into the depths – where I would almost certainly pass out. Too much, and I'd go up too quickly, and I'd get

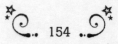

the bends. And you don't want to get the bends, trust me. You get gas bubbles in your system; it's painful, it's scary, and people have died from it.

On the other hand, I had to compensate for the force that was pulling me down, or else I wasn't going anywhere. Plus, I had to think ahead; once I was free of the whirlpool, I might shoot up really fast if I over-compensated. Ty looked worried; I could see him trying to get near me, probably to fix the pressure himself, but the forces were against him. Slowly, slowly, I let in more air…yes! Now I could feel a little bit of a lift, and I was face down, drifting away.

Again I saw Quaid. For some reason I guess I'd expected to see one of those treasure chests beside him, like you get in comics…but I realised now that this was really dumb. Even if the jewels had been stored in anything like that, the timbers would have rotted away long ago, just as the ship itself would have done. I shone my torch instead on the rocks beside him, where I thought I saw something glitter…yes! Here and there, sharp glints flashing, all around him. They *had* to be diamonds…didn't they? Still the foul circus was parading round me, following me up, but I could feel their force weakening. I could still see the glittering jewels, but I was much too far away to reach them – and I was never

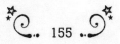

going to get any closer now. Captain Quaid's ghostly guards would see to that.

*Stupid!* What use were they to him? He was dead! Some of these ghosts and their obsessions…honestly! So crazy, so dumb.

I floated, waiting. Giving my system a chance to adjust to the change in pressure before the next climb. Relief; the horrible faces were falling away now…and away, and away…

Now Ty was beside me, and Sam. We held onto each other and breathed. I could no longer see the glittering horde…had no idea whether Ty had seen it or caught it on camera.

Up again we went, another stage.

*Breathe.*

Though the waters were still turbulent, we were out of danger now.

Finally, we headed back to the boat.

The reception we got from Maro, Sean and Phoebe was like royalty; Maro, in particular, went berserk. As for me, I couldn't wait to tell them what I'd seen – but I was beaten to it.

'It's incredible!' gasped Ty, waving his camera. 'Did you catch all that on the monitor? I think this is a really important find.'

'You saw them?' I said. 'You got pictures?'

'Saw what?' asked Maro. 'I'm not sure what I was looking at.'

'Diamonds,' I said. 'Exactly what I thought would be there; diamonds and pearls. And there'll be other stuff down there as well; it's the wreck of the *Venus*. We've found the wreck of the *Venus*!'

The sun was setting when we arrived in the village. Ty was still with us; Sean had dropped us off, on his way back to the house. He was all excited, saying he had to make a bunch of phone calls about the discovery. Phoebe and Maro had gone with him.

Ty had asked loads of questions. We didn't give in to the pressure, but Ashley did mention that we hoped to help Bill – who he knew – and that he was the one who had helped us find the jewels.

'Oh, I can't wait to tell Bill about this!' I cried, as we tripped up the stone steps towards his cottage.

'Don't overdo it, Kitty,' insisted Ty. 'Remember just to say we *might* have found something important. We won't know for sure until we find a way to access the site.'

'Yeah, I know,' I said, not really listening. 'And it's all thanks to him. Yay! We're gonna make him rich!'

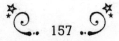

'*Might*,' said Ty.

Funnily enough, Ashley seemed just as excited as I was by now. 'Bill!' we both cried, as we got near. 'Hey, Bill!'

Not seeing him in the courtyard, we made our way across the obstacle course to his front door and knocked. 'Hey, Bill!'

We waited. He didn't come to the door.

There were no lights on inside.

'Does anyone have a phone number for him?' asked Ty.

'Mum might,' said Ashley. 'I think she may still have my old school class list in a drawer somewhere.'

'But he's not home,' Flossie pointed out.

Ty, meanwhile, was marching around, trying to get a signal on his phone to call Phoebe.

'Maybe there'll be a mobile number,' suggested Sam.

Ty got hold of Phoebe, but she wasn't home yet.

'Maybe he's gone to the pub,' said Sam. 'Does anyone know what pub he goes to?'

'I do,' said Ty. 'Good idea; we could try that. Come on.'

We turned and headed back into the village. In all the excitement, I stumbled on one of the stone steps; it wasn't till we'd gone a bit further that I noticed

something missing. I felt in my pocket. 'Hang on; where's my phone?'

'Maybe it fell out of your pocket back there, where you tripped,' suggested Flossie.

'I'll go have a look.' I turned and headed back up the steps; yes, there it was. I bent to pick it up, and as I looked up I caught a glimpse of some movement through the window of Bill's place. *Weird*, I thought. I crept closer, keeping low. The window was on the other side of the cottage from the courtyard, where the bins were kept. I sneaked right up close, and allowed myself a nanosecond's glimpse inside. It was enough for me to see that yes; it was Bill. He *was* home!

I made my way back to the others. 'Guys!' I hissed. 'Bill *is* in! He's hiding.'

'Hiding?' repeated Ashley. 'Why?'

'I don't know.'

'Is he alone?' asked Ty.

'I don't know, I couldn't tell…I think so. He seemed to be…I dunno, sort of pacing about.'

'That's weird,' said Ashley. 'He was really friendly this morning. And what if we were coming to give him news of Megan? We said we'd be on the lookout.'

'Something must have happened since then,' I said. I went back and knocked again. 'Bill, it's Ashley and

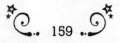

Kitty here, and we've got some amazing news! Please, we really need to talk to you…we've found the remains of the *Venus*!'

We all huddled at the front door, listening.

'Bill, we know you're in there,' said Ashley. 'Please open the door. This is really important, Bill!'

We stood and waited. Finally, after a few moments, there was the sound of bolts being unlocked. The door opened just a little way, with the chain still on; Bill's unshaven face appeared. He looked tired, and his silver hair was all mussed up.

'Bill, it's true,' I said. 'We've found the *Venus*! At least, we've found its treasure. We've got pictures and everything!'

Ty held up his camera; Bill nodded slightly.

'*Please* let us come in.'

The door shut again; there was the sound of the chain being slid out, then the door opened up properly. Bill stood aside.

'Bill, what's the matter?' asked Ashley, as we headed into the stuffy, gloomy little room.

'Oh, I'm just not feelin' too great, is all,' said Bill. He hesitated. 'And…I'm worried now. 'Bout Megan. I got a hunch, see…a bad feeling in me gut. I've even went an' called the police.'

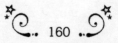

I felt my heart sink. Even though I could tell she hadn't been planning to go back to her dad like we'd told her to, this felt ominous now. 'Oh, uh, really?'

'Yeah, only now I'm wishin' I hadn't. I'm worried I might've made things worse...'

OK, so he knew Megan was probably involved in something illegal. And yet at the same time, he was worrying himself sick – didn't know what else to do but call the police. Where *was* she?

'Wait, Megan's your daughter, right?' said Ty. 'What happened? Is she missing? I don't understand...why would calling the police make things worse?'

We all looked at each other, dumbstruck. *Great*, I thought; we really should have explained to Ty beforehand.

'N-no, she's not missing,' said Ashley. 'I mean...that is...' She trailed off, staring at the floor, clearly not wanting to say anything about what had happened that afternoon.

*Oh jeez*, I thought; I'd really gone and landed us in it now. It was time to come clean. 'What Ashley's trying to say is that we've seen her,' I admitted.

'You have?' said Bill, wide-eyed.

'Yes. But...earlier on today – about three-ish, three-fifteen. We told her you were worried about her...we

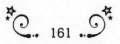

161

said she needed to come home. But, uh, she hasn't and…well, we have no more idea than you about where she might be now.'

Suddenly, Bill's face was like thunder. 'Well, where was she? Who was she with?'

'I…uh…you see…' I dried up. I felt terrible now.

'OK, I don't like the sound of this,' said Ty. 'We have to find this girl. Number one priority.'

# Raid

'But we were worried we'd make things even worse!' cried Ashley. 'Just like Bill!'

She was sobbing her heart out, and having a screaming row with her big brother, now that we'd had to tell him the whole story about Megan. He was furious with her – with us *all* – for not having reported the criminal activity we'd witnessed straight away.

'The worst thing you could do, was do nothing!' yelled Ty, as we headed back down into the village. 'And now…who knows what's happened to her!'

'We *didn't* do nothing!' cried Ashley. 'This whole thing with the *Venus*, and the treasure…Kitty knew. She knew! This is what was going to *save* Megan; don't you see?'

'Yeah, and meanwhile we've been losing precious time,' said Ty.

I was trembling with emotion. 'It's not her fault!' I blurted out.

Ty blinked at me.

'Look, if this is anyone's fault it's mine, not Ashley's,' I went on, my face prickling with heat. 'It's just… I thought I saw a way of helping Megan and her dad without getting her into trouble.'

'That's all very well, but you still should have reported what you saw,' said Ty.

'But to be fair to Kitty, we wouldn't even know about *any* of this if it wasn't for her,' said Sam. 'She spotted Megan the other day, being bullied by someone.'

'Yeah, if something bad's happened to Megan, it would've happened anyway,' said Ashley, 'and could've happened at any time.'

'It's true,' I said. 'Megan's been involved with these smugglers for quite a while now, judging from…well, something Bill said, actually. And they treat her terribly.'

'And you can put your hand on your heart and say that you've done nothing to stir things up?' asked Ty.

I blinked at him. 'Well…I…'

*Could* I?

I thought back to the afternoon; our snooping at the cove, our discussion with Megan at Bosreath Cove.

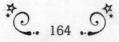

Surely no one could have seen that…could they? No: we were able to see in every direction; there was no one. And that Howie guy, over at the smugglers' cove: he couldn't have seen or heard us the whole time we were outside the cave, or he'd have come after us. We were quiet as mice when we left, too – except…

*Oh no.*

Except when Beth appeared.

Had Howie heard me cry out? Had he come out of the cave and glimpsed us before we disappeared into the tunnel? My heart raced. But hang on: that was before Megan had left him. If he'd heard me, she'd have known about it – and she hadn't said anything. *Would* she have told us, though? Surely she would…

My thoughts were going round in circles. 'I really don't think so,' I said at last.

'Right, well we've just got to do what we can to help now,' said Ty.

By this time we were down in the village; the streetlights were coming on.

'Maybe her friends can help us find her,' suggested Sam. 'That gang she hangs out with.'

'Hmm…well, I don't see them. Where might they be?'

'Never mind them,' said Ty. 'That's the first thing

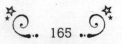

the police will have done – they know those guys. Are there any leads you have, that the police might not? What about the person you saw bullying her on the cliff?'

'Well, the main thing I remember is, he wore a long black leather coat.'

'Oh, I know where *he* lives,' said Flossie.

My jaw nearly hit the ground. 'You do?'

'Yeah. I saw him come out of his house a couple of times, when Maro an' I were going to the pottery place – you know, where Phoebe helps out? You guys were doing your diving course.'

'You never said anything!'

'Why should I?'

'Well, the coat…'

'You never *said* anything about the coat,' said Flossie.

'I didn't?'

'Uh-uh. Not till now.'

'Hang on,' said Ty, 'how do you know it's him? You're basing this on a *coat*?'

'A black *leather* coat, Ty,' I said. 'Ankle-length. How many people do you see around Pelporth in one of those?'

'OK,' said Ty. 'Where does this guy live?'

'There's a cut-through from the car park,' said

Flossie, pointing to the hill behind the village. 'It's up there.'

Now it was completely dark. Ty had called the police, and they were on their way. They'd told Bill; he'd said he would stay put, and wait for any news. The police told us to meet them in the car park, then show them where the house was; it wasn't accessible by car, and of course Flossie didn't have an address. The quickest way up to the car park from the village was a narrow cutting from behind the church; just mud steps with wooden supports. It was a popular haunt for several Pelporth ghosts, which was a royal pain in the bum for me, I'm not gonna lie. Honestly, there were times I really wished I could just turn my phantorama off. At least Beth wasn't bugging me right now…not yet, anyway.

Finally, near the top of the hill, the footpath crossed an alleyway lined with a row of little cottages.

'It's here,' said Flossie. 'Down that way,' she added, pointing.

'Which one, Floss?' asked Sam. 'Do you remember?'

'Well, it's the yellow one…only…I can't see the colours now. It's too dark.'

'Never mind, we'll find it,' said Ty. 'C'mon, let's get to the car park.'

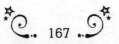

We turned right and continued on the path as it led us through the woods to the car park…then something made us stop dead in our tracks.

A scream.

We stared at each other, eyes gleaming. 'C'mon!' said Ty, breaking into a run.

'There isn't time!' cried Flossie. 'It's like, five more minutes to the car park from here.'

Ty got out his phone. 'Then we'll direct them to us…hello?'

We stood there in the dark while he made the call. 'We just heard a scream,' he said. 'No time to come to the car park…just come to the row of cottages, you'll find us…OK…thanks.'

We turned and dashed back towards the cottages. 'If we work out which one it is, we just lay low till they get here – see what we can see.'

The alleyway was deserted. Rainbow TV screens flickered through net curtains; had the scream come from one of them?

'That one, there,' said Flossie suddenly, pointing to the next cottage ahead of us. No lights on in the front rooms – but on the ground floor you could just make out a soft glow from further inside somewhere. And I could hear voices – male and female, arguing.

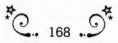

I felt myself gripped by panic, but thank god, the next moment I heard pounding footsteps and police walkie-talkies. 'Ty Goodstow?' said the older one.

'Yes,' said Ty. 'That's the cottage, there – right, Flossie?' Flossie nodded.

'All right,' said the policeman. 'I'll need to get some more details from you – wait here, please.' Then he pounded on the door. 'Police! Open up!'

Silence.

A flicking of net curtains next door. Then the front door opened and an old lady in an aqua blue housecoat peered out. 'Anything I can help with, officers?'

'Can we go through your house?' asked Cop Senior.

She nodded, making way for them.

'If you don't want to wait, you can meet us back at the station,' Cop Junior told us. 'But we do need to talk to you.' They thanked the lady and thundered down her tiny hallway. In all the excitement, the lady followed them, without closing the door.

Yep: the door was *ajar*. No way was I going to wait out here! I sneaked in.

'No, Kitty!' Ty came after me, but I shot through the dinky little pink-and-beige home in no time minus five. Out the back, the old lady was standing in her garden, her head craning to catch as much of the action as

possible. 'Oh no, dear, I don't think–' she began as she saw me, but I just said, 'Sorry,' as I clambered over the low hedge bordering the two back gardens.

Next door, I saw that the police had apparently already forced open the sliding glass patio door, and a man's voice protested: 'What the hell do you think you're doing?'

I hid beside the patio doorway; Ty and the others came up beside me. Now that we were here, he didn't try to drag us away – hey, he was probably just as keen to know what was going on.

I could see the man, standing there in the kitchen: neat, dark hair, just like the one I'd seen with Megan before…other than that, I couldn't tell if it was the same guy. No leather coat! Well, he'd hardly be wearing it indoors, would he?

Cop Senior held up his ID. 'We have reason to believe a missing child is on the premises – Megan Magwithan.'

The man leaned against the breakfast bar. 'I don't know why you would think that,' he said. 'I don't know any Megan Magwithan. I live alone; it's just me here.'

'And your name is…?'

'Aidan Kernon,' said the man.

'Well Mr Kernon, we understand she's been seen

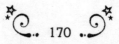

170

with you,' said the policeman. 'And just now we heard a scream.'

'A scream? Not from here, you didn't,' said Kernon. Now he seemed more relaxed – he even smiled a bit.

'And there were voices, Mr Kernon.'

'Oh…voices? Well, I was watching telly, wasn't I? That's what you heard! Yeah, and there was a scream an' all, now I think of it.'

He was lying, I knew it. I could see through the open-plan kitchen into the living room: huge TV mounted over the fireplace. I'd sure as hell have noticed *that* from outside if it had been on.

The policeman wasn't fooled either; he went over, picked up the remote and zapped the TV on: a cookery programme. He turned to Kernon. 'All right. Where is she?'

Kernon still wasn't fazed. 'That would've just started,' he said casually. He consulted his watch. 'It's just gone eight-thirty.'

Cop Senior narrowed his eyes at him. Just as things were getting interesting, we were rumbled: Cop Junior spotted us. 'Hey you! I thought I told you to wait outside.'

'Oh, yeah, well–'

'What the hell…?' said Kernon, turning to us. 'Get those kids outta here!'

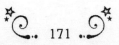

'It's OK, they're going,' said Cop Junior. 'Come on – out!' He hurried us along, indicating that we go through the house to the front door.

Fine – but that didn't mean I couldn't look for a sign of Megan along the way. Not much in the way of hiding places, I noticed…but there was one thing I realised would be a *big* clue: her sopping wet shoes. I scanned the wooden floor as I went, taking my time…

'Oh!' I said, pointing to a damp patch near the cooker. 'That's odd. The floor's all wet there.' I caught Cop Senior's eye. 'I WONDER WHY THAT IS.' It hadn't rained all day.

'I spilt something,' said Kernon, through gritted teeth. 'Not every day you get broken into: bit of a *shock*, you know? I'll see you out.'

As he motioned towards the front door, Cop Senior held him back – no doubt thinking he'd try to do a runner. 'No need, sir. I think they can find their own way out.'

'Oh, it's just the door's a bit stiff,' said Kernon.

'My colleague has dealt with plenty of stiff doors in his time – right, Harry?'

Cop Junior nodded as he guided us through. 'Yup, no worries.'

'All right, look…you'll need these,' said Kernon,

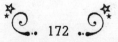

pulling a bunch of keys from his pocket. He looked around, reading our thoughts. 'I always lock it at night. Security.'

Cop Senior gazed at him for several seconds. 'Is that so?'

'Yeah.' Kernon was more uncomfortable now: sweat glistened on his upper lip.

'Funny, that,' said Cop Senior. 'Just now you said the door was...*stiff*. Lot of break-ins around Pelporth, are there? Harry, you aware of a lot of break-ins around here?'

'Can't say as I am, sir.'

'*Habit*,' said Kernon hastily. 'I used to live in London.' He chucked the keys to young Harry. 'It's the brass one.'

'Thanks.' Harry caught the keys and led us out into the hall.

Well, I wasn't ready to give up on finding Megan yet. As I got to the banister – with, I noticed, that leather coat hanging on it – I quickly doubled back up the stairs.

Cop Junior bounded up after me...I lurched forward and dived into the first room I came to – the bathroom. The policeman grabbed my arm. 'Come along now, you have to leave this to us.'

'Wait! I just–' Tugging myself away from him,

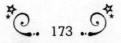

I knocked the lid off the laundry hamper and there, slung on top of the dirty clothes, was a pair of soggy, falling-apart Keds: Megan's. I grabbed them. 'Look! These are hers...and she got them wet today!'

'All right,' said the policeman. 'Megan? We know you're here...come on out now, please!'

Together we slammed into the front bedroom. The first thing I noticed was that the window was open, its stay dangling. 'She's gone!' I cried. I dashed over and looked out; no sign of her, but it wouldn't have been too hard for her to climb out because the cottage was small, and had a bay window...

I turned to speak to Harry, but he was already gone.

# Finding Jed

I ran downstairs, and out the front of the house:
I couldn't see much, but I could hear Megan's voice, and
within a moment or two I saw the huddled figures of
her and the young policeman coming back towards the
cottage. Megan had been protesting, but it hadn't lasted;
now she just hung her head as she slunk back in her bare
feet, held protectively by Cop Junior. The lady in the
aqua housecoat was outside her front door again,
shaking her head. A police siren screamed through
the air…

Down at the police station, Bill turned up, looking grim
as stone. Megan sat with her hair in front of her face,
barely glanced at him. We got interviewed by three
different police teams in separate rooms: Kernon with
one, Megan and Bill with another, and the rest of us

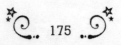

together. They asked us how we knew what Megan was up to, what exactly we'd seen and heard…all of that.

At the end we got a bit of chat about well done, kids, blah blah – but all done in that way that you know what's coming next: and by the way, if you're thinking of ever going back to the smugglers' cove – don't. OK? Because it's a REALLY DUMB THING TO DO. Yeah? Dangerous.

Later, we got the full story: Megan confessed all. About how Kernon and Howie were a team, bringing in fake designer jewellery and watches by boat from overseas. Somehow the stuff needed to be distributed around the country – but they couldn't risk transferring big loads of the stuff from cave to vehicle, even at such a remote location; it had to be moved in small amounts, and on foot. That was where poor Megan came in. Back and forth, back and forth with her rucksack, sometimes to Kernon in his car (always at a different spot), sometimes by train to Bristol, dodging fares, being paid just enough 'pocket money' to keep her coming back for more.

Until, that is, we came along. We'd rescued her; yay! Hurray for us!

Well, sort of.

Actually, it turned out it was my fault that she'd not gone home after we saw her at the cove. 'Howie heard someone cry out,' Megan explained, after her interview was finished.

'Oh,' I said, looking at the floor. That was me, of course – when Beth appeared.

'He was worried someone had seen us,' said Megan. 'And straight away he thought it were to do with me, you know? Like I'd had enough, was going to give the whole game away. So he called Aidan. Well, I weren't letting on; I said there weren't nobody there. Said it was a seagull. But Howie had told him he thought he'd seen someone as well and, oh… I'm sorry, Dad. I'd have bin home ages by now, but Aidan, he wouldn't let up about it, locked the front door an' everything…well, you know about that.'

I felt terrible that she'd had to go through all that because of me. Being locked in and everything…like a prisoner! Urgh, that Beth Trewin! If she hadn't loomed up at me unexpectedly like that, I wouldn't have cried out, and none of this would have happened. Man, she was hacking me off now! I needed to sort her out once and for all.

'I'm just so glad you're all right,' said Bill, giving Megan a hug.

That really opened the floodgates. 'I'm sorry, Dad,' she sobbed. 'I just…well, both of us, we…we just *really needed the money*. I wanted to help yoo-hooo!'

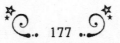

I bit my lip, looked away. I tried to imagine what that was like for her. Would I be any better in those circumstances?

Anyway, now that we'd given our witness statements, we were free to go. We saw Aidan Kernon on our way out: apparently he was refusing to say anything, insisting he should have a lawyer present. Meanwhile the police were collecting a whole team to go and search the smugglers' cove, and to track down Howie.

'I hope Megan doesn't get into too much trouble,' I said, as we wove our way back through the narrow streets.

'Yeah, me too,' said Ashley.

'Really?' I said; I was pretty surprised, given how judgmental she'd been before about her.

Ashley sighed. 'Yeah, really. I…I feel bad now. The way she wouldn't let on about us to Aidan, even under all that pressure? That was good of her, I have to say. She didn't need to do that.'

'Yeah,' said Sam.

'Not only that,' I said, 'it makes you realise something about bullies.'

'What?' asked Ty.

'That sometimes the bully is a victim too, ' I said. 'Megan bullied Ashley back in year six; now here she is,

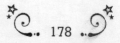

being bullied herself, by Aidan Kernon.'

'Kitty, you can hardly compare a bit of playground teasing with coercing someone into crime,' said Ty.

'No, I get what she means,' said Ashley. 'And she has a point. See, before, all I saw in Megan was someone who'd been mean to me. And yeah, a dropout…a loser. It wouldn't have occurred to me in a million years that she might be any kind of victim herself.'

'Don't be too hard on yourself, Ashley,' said Ty. His voice had softened; I was glad to see he wasn't mad at her – or the rest of us – any more. It didn't stop him reminding us (one of those 'gentle' reminders grown-ups go in for that's really just a telling-off minus the actual shouting) that we'd been wrong not to report the incident down at the cove right away. As if we needed reminding! We'd been just as freaked out as he was when Megan went AWOL.

Anyway.

I did allow myself a little pat on the back, for *noticing* that there was bad-bordering-on-outright-nasty stuff going down with Megan in the first place. Well, that was her sorted out – for now, at least. But as for Beth…her timing was lousy, and I hadn't had a chance to explain anything to her. Her Unfinished Business was still unfinished, and I was meant to finish it for her. I would

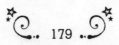

have to try to summon her: there was so much to tell! I was still trying to pull everything together in my mind, but there had been a lot of progress. I had to tell her about the discovery of the jewels, and Quaid... She needed to know all this stuff. But I suddenly realised I was starving; before I did anything, I was going in for dinner.

'Beth? Beth!' I called, my voice whipping up in the wind around the ancient stones.

The moon was rising now – a full moon, but still low in the sky with clouds scudding across it. It was all I had for light. I'd sneaked out after we'd all got back to the house, saying I was going to the Hippo. Then I'd made my way back up to the Logan Stone. I was so shattered I could barely move – but this couldn't wait. For one thing, Beth needed bringing under control. The stupid tricks with the seaweed and the fish, the constant badgering, the turning up at the cove and who knew, maybe nearly getting us killed... For another, she needed to understand that I might actually have discovered a way of reuniting her with Jed.

'Beth!' I cried, as I climbed up and sat beside the Logan Stone. Instinctively, I rested my hand on it; I never could resist just checking to see if it would move

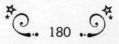

– if, according to the old legend, I was somehow now 'pure of spirit'. Needless to say, the stone didn't move. *I'm still as wicked as ever, I guess*, I thought. I shut my eyes, and called to her from deep inside me: *Come to me, Beth Trewin! Come to me now…*

I thought I would have to work hard at enticing her to this spot, which was not a regular haunt for her. As it turned out, I didn't have to.

'My Jed!' said a voice. I opened my eyes, and there she stood on the rocks opposite me, pale and faint in the moonlight. 'Ee'm found my Jed! 'Tis th'only reason ee would be callin' me here.' Her eyes shone as she gazed around. 'My Jed! Where he be?'

'No, you don't understand,' I said. 'I haven't found him – not yet. And what's more, neither of us is ever going to find him in this world. But–'

Beth threw back her head and howled.

'Look, but…hey, I said in *this* world. I need to explain something to you…'

Beth wasn't listening. 'Ee'm never going to find 'im! And now ee'm brung me 'ere to tell me it's the *E-HE-HEND!*' She launched into another long howl, mouth stretched into an ugly grimace, ghost-snot streaming down her face.

'No, please, you've got to listen to me! Oh…here,'

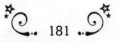

I pulled a tissue out of my pocket and handed it to her – only then did it strike me that ghosts probably didn't use Kleenex. 'I mean, er…'

Ghost or not, Beth grabbed the tissue and blew her nose. She blew so hard, her face sort of imploded into the tissue, and for a moment it looked as if all the rest of her was going to disappear into it as well. Then her face reformed itself, and she handed the tissue back, completely drenched in greenish slime. Eew! I backed away, letting it fall to the ground. It fizzled into nothing.

'Owoowoowoo!' Beth cried on.

'LOOK, ABOUT JED,' I yelled over the racket. 'What I'm *trying* to tell you is, I think I've discovered something important—'

'If it ent my Jed ee'm discovered, I'll not want to kno-ho-how,' sobbed Beth.

'BUT I'M *GOING* TO FIND HIM!' I shouted.

Beth fell silent, ghost-snot streaming down her face. *Finally!*

'Good, thank you,' I said. 'Now, just be quiet for a minute and I'll explain. It has to do with Captain Quaid. I think he's the reason you're stuck here, in the mortal realm. He's guarding the jewels, down where the *Venus* was sunk. He's a powerful spirit – a Grade A – you know, you saw how he destroyed your ship.'

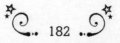

'Ay, that were 'im, all right,' said Beth, furiously.

'Well, he's still powerful,' I said. 'So powerful, he can cause people to have visions of the *Venus*, and be hypnotised by it so they have fatal accidents. But look, it's all about the jewels. Now, I can't promise anything, but if we can—'

'Can't promise anything!' snapped Beth. 'So ee LIED just now, when ee said ee were going to find Jed!'

'No, I didn't!' God, she was really doing my head in now. It hadn't been a lie – well, OK, it was a sort-of-half-truth. But I'd said it because it seemed like the only way I could shut her up. 'Look…' For a moment, I was lost for words. I wanted to give her a cast-iron guarantee, but I couldn't. 'OK, you know what?' I said at last. 'I know where Jed is: he's waiting for you, over on the other side.' To be honest I still didn't know this for a fact, but it was the most logical explanation.

'On the other side…?'

'Yes. He's in…' I trailed off. Where? Heaven? Hell? Purgatory? How would I know? 'The spirit world,' I said at last. 'So just go back to him, now. Then you can stop bugging me with all the fishy nonsense, and turning up, having a go at me – *which*, by the way, put me in some serious danger today. And my brother and sister, too!'

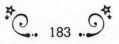

'But I can't!' wailed Beth. 'I know not how!'

'Just…relax. Let yourself go. Do some…I dunno, meditation or something.'

'Medi-what?' said Beth.

I sighed loudly. '*Meditation*; it's emptying your head of all thoughts.' Blimey…I couldn't actually believe this conversation. But if I wanted to test my theory that it was Quaid who was keeping her trapped in the mortal realm, this was a worthwhile experiment. 'You'll find him,' I said, 'because you are emotionally connected. He's there, waiting for you!' *God, Kitty, what a load of rubbish*, I thought. I mean, it sort of *felt* like it would be true – and people always believe they'll be reunited with loved ones, don't they? But who was I to say what would really happen? It wasn't as if I'd ever done any actual dying.

My phone rang; I saw on the screen it was Maro. Which probably meant she'd gone to the Hippo, and found me not there. Eek.

'I've got to go,' I said, pocketing my phone and scrambling down from the rock.

'Wait!' called Beth, swooping down after me. 'I know not what to do.'

'All right!' I said, turning to face her. 'Look, it's just as I thought: you can't go over to the other side, because

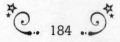

184

a force more powerful than your own will is keeping you here. And I'm more sure than ever now that that force is Quaid. So I'll tell you what to do: just give me more time. And that means *leaving me alone*, understand? No pestering, no fishy business…nothing. I'm onto something here, but *I* will come to *you* when it's time. OK? I mean, all right?'

Beth gazed this way and that, as if searching for an answer. 'All right, so be it,' she said at last, then faded away.

I sighed deeply, then headed back to the house. *Whoom!* There was Beth again, standing in my way. 'Ee promise, now?'

'Jesus! Yes, I promise!'

I continued on my way, then once again she appeared: 'Ee'll not forget?'

*Man*, some ghosts were persistent! I flung out my arms in exasperation. 'Beth, I won't forget, but if you do that one more time, I'll, I'll…'

'Very well!' she said quickly, and then *poof!* she was gone for good.

# Charms and Incantations

What with all the drama surrounding Megan, we hadn't actually had a chance to talk to Bill about our exciting underwater discovery. And it was important that we did, because in a few days' time we'd be going out again – and this time we were going to need his help.

So Ashley, Ty and I paid them a visit.

'How's Megan?' asked Ashley.

'Ah, she's sleeping right now,' said Bill. 'She's just very tired, y'know? But otherwise OK, I s'pose, considerin'. I hear they got the other fella.'

'Howie, yes,' I said. 'They're both locked up now.'

'But they'll get reduced sentences if they give the police any other names,' added Ty.

'Oh, they done that,' said Bill. 'Gave 'em one, over in France. Some supplier.'

'No one else, then?' I asked, remembering what

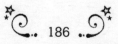

Megan had said down at Bosreath Bay, about how trapped she felt because of the whole network of criminals Aidan and Howie belonged to.

'No one else,' said Bill. 'Megan reckons they used to talk about all these heavies they knew, so's to scare her. But then where were they when the fella was trying to get information out of 'er, eh?'

*Good point,* I thought.

'Nah,' Bill went on. 'Anyone else involved, they'd want their cut, and these fellas, they're too greedy to share. An' I knows all about greed, let me tell yer...'

'Yes, well–' Ty began.

But Bill was off on a rant. 'It's the whole reason I'm out o' work, y'know? Greedy supermarket bosses, don't see it worth their while dealin' with the small-time fisherman, when they can just...'

I couldn't just sit there politely any longer: I was bursting. 'Bill, I'm sorry, this probably didn't sink in last time, but, um, see, we found the wreck of the *Venus*!'

Bill's pale blue eyes widened. 'Oh my lord, yes, so you did! Sorry, slipped me mind, what with everything...'

'Yes, of course...'

'Well, congratulations! Fantastic! How'd you manage that, then?'

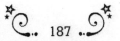

'It was you, Bill,' I said. 'You told us exactly where to look.'

Bill frowned. 'I did?'

'Yes, you showed us the place on the map,' I said. 'The no-go zone?'

'There? You've got to be kiddin' me!'

'She's not,' said Ty. 'Boy, I don't know what it is, but you're absolutely right, Bill; there's something very weird going on in the waters there. Never seen anything like it!'

'Ain't a no-go zone for no reason,' said Bill. 'You gets yer blighted spots on land, ain't no reason wouldn't be the same at sea. Spirits o' the deep, an' all that – don't be messin' with 'em.'

'Spirits of the deep?' said Ty, glancing at me. Clearly, the whole family knew by now that this was all about ghosts. But did Bill?

'Oh, mermaids, selkies, call 'em what yer will,' said Bill. 'They's spirits, an' no mistakin'.'

'Well, whatever they are,' said Ty, 'I wish there was a way of calming them down long enough for us to explore the site properly. This is going to be very tricky.'

'You might be able to, if you work hard enough at it,' said Bill. 'There's charms an' so on.'

'Charms?'

'You know: incantations.'

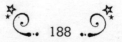

Ty laughed. 'I wouldn't know the first thing about anything like that!'

'Ah,' said Bill, with a wink. 'But I do. This here, for example. See this?' He took a stone from his dusty mantelpiece. 'It's me milpreve – me lucky stone. Always used to take it out with me if the weather were threatenin' to turn.'

He handed it to Ashley. It was a little smaller than a tennis ball, whitish in colour, with a couple of holes running right through it.

'That's coralline limestone, isn't it?' said Ty, peering at it.

'Somethin' like that,' said Bill. 'I wouldn't be without it. Or this,' he added, leaning forward as he showed us a silver pendant around his neck. 'That's me Saint Andrew, see? I prays to 'im when I'm needing assistance in calming the waters.'

I remembered Bill talking about calling on the help of the saints before, but I hadn't really taken it seriously.

Ty smiled and nodded: I could see he thought the same, but probably figured hey, whatever it takes. He'd had a hard time believing what he saw happening in the waters of the no-go zone; there was no logical explanation for that, either – but it was real. 'Well, can you come out with us on Thursday?' he asked. 'We've

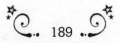

had an amazing stroke of luck – a friend of Dad's is one of the world's top shipwreck recovery specialists, and he just happens to be in Cornwall for a few days before heading off to South Africa. He's insanely busy, but he's making time in his schedule. So what do you think? Thursday?'

Bill nodded. 'Will do. Reckon the weather'll be fine then, too. Wind's mellowin', I believe.'

'Excellent,' said Ty, shaking his hand. 'We're on!'


Well, the wind didn't mellow. It got distinctly un-mellow, i.e. blustery, grey and squally. Out to sea, the choppy waves were tipped with white foam.

But today was the day of the expedition – and it had to be today. We went to pick Bill up on the way. Ashley and I huddled in our anoraks as we hurried up the path to the cottage.

'It's not exactly what the forecast said, is it?' I said.

Ashley shrugged. 'No such thing as forecasting in Cornwall.'

We knocked on Bill's door.

Bill appeared, still in his slippers. 'You're not thinkin' of goin' out in this, are yer?'

'We have to,' I said. 'It's the only day that specialist can come – remember?'

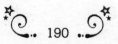

Bill gazed out, shook his head and tutted. 'Sorry, but I think we'd better leave it for today, if it's all the same to you. Maybe tomorrow, eh?'

'But we can't do it tomorrow!' I cried. 'It has to be today. We've got the whole team together, and the guy's going to South Africa, he's gonna be gone, like six months…we need you! You're the only one who can calm the waters in the no-go zone!'

'Well, I didn't say I *could*,' said Bill. 'Only that I *might*. But…not today.'

I felt as if the ground was falling away below me. Everything hung on this: we needed Bill with his specialist seafaring knowledge, his charms and incantations…these were *sea* spirits we were dealing with, and I for one was ready to believe that Bill might just calm them. I knew *I* wouldn't be able to – and I needed to get this curse lifted now, today, before it was too late. Before someone else fell victim to the thirty-year cycle of *Venus* sightings. And what was Quaid, once you took his treasure away from him? Nothing. His spirit would be defeated, and a defeated spirit would lose the power to destroy other people's lives. And Beth would be released.

Well, in theory.

To be honest I had no idea if it would actually work

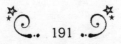

out like that, but the theory was all I had to cling to, and by now I was clinging to it like a barnacle.

Bill wasn't budging. 'Truth is, I'm a bit poorly,' he said. 'It's me rheumatism, y'know. But you'll manage without me. Here: you can borrow my milpreve, if you want.'

'No!' said Ashley. 'Please, Bill. It's *you* we need.'

'We haven't got your expertise!' I added, probably sounding desperate by now.

'Go, Dad,' came a voice from inside; Megan appeared. 'You can't let them down, not now.'

'Oh, hi,' I said, still sounding a bit shrill. I lowered my voice. 'Are you...is everything...?' I didn't really know what to say.

'I'm going to court,' said Megan. 'But it's nothing terrible. I'm to get one o' these YRO things – youth rehabilitation order. They do bazillions of assessments, keep tabs on you, make you go to school an' stuff. So I've got to be on Best Behaviour; can't really see anyone right now.'

*The gang*, I thought: her crowd of waster friends.

'Oh.' I didn't know what else to say.

'It's OK, you know,' she added. 'I don't blame you for what's happened.'

'Oh! I didn't know whether...I mean yeah, we

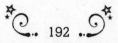

rescued you and all that. But all that trouble over at Aidan's…that wouldn't have happened if it wasn't for us. Well, me.'

Megan shrugged. 'Something like it would've happened sooner or later. You did me a favour.'

'Well, we'll be doing you an even bigger one, if only we can get your dad to come out on the boat with us,' said Ashley.

Megan frowned. 'Doing me a favour? I don't understand…' She turned to Bill, searching for an answer.

'Oh!' I said. This seemed to be virtually my entire vocabulary right now: different kinds of 'oh'. 'So you don't know…'

'I might get a small reward,' Bill explained to Megan.

'Small reward!' said Ashley. 'But—' The rest of her remark was drowned out by the honking of Sean's horn.

'Just go,' said Megan, parking Bill's wellies on the doormat for him. 'I'll be fine.'

'But the weather isn't!' Bill protested.

'You've been out in worse,' said Megan. She turned to us. 'He's making excuses. The truth is, he doesn't want to leave me alone, not for a minute. Now go, Dad!'

Bill looked at Megan, then us, then the sky, then the wellies. His red-rimmed eyes looked ready to fill with tears. 'I…I…'

There was an awkward silence. I thought of Megan having to sit there alone in the cottage, not being able to see her mates…probably bored out of her brains, and tempted to sneak out. No wonder Bill didn't want to let her out of his sight.

Then Ashley stepped forward. '*I'll* stay with you.'

Well. I was gobsmacked.

'You what?' said Megan, a cynical smile twisting her lips.

'Well, y'know, only if you *want*,' said Ashley sharply.

'That's actually a really good idea,' I said. 'If it makes you feel better, Bill…?'

'Well, yes, I s'pose it would,' said Bill.

'Then it's cool, Dad,' said Megan. 'So go on. No excuse now, eh?'

Sean honked again.

Bill sighed at his boots. 'All right, then. Here goes.'

# 20

# Circle of Spirits

Thick grey cloud hung over us like God's duvet.

Far off in the distance there was brightness glimmering on the water, but here it was all turmoil and sea-spray. And we weren't even there yet.

All that rolling around was pretty stomach-churning. At least Maro wasn't with us this time – she wouldn't have lasted five minutes. The rest of Cornwall was out here with us, though – or at least it felt that way. There was our boat, followed by this whacking great thing full of shipwreck recovery people. Then there were the surveillance people, and some newspaper people who'd been tipped off that something big was going down. Four boats in all.

'Too many of 'em,' grumbled Bill, shaking his head. 'Like a blimmin' circus.' He patted his pockets. 'Where's me baccy? Oh, blast...anyone got any baccy? All these folk, they're makin' me nervous.'

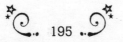

No one had any tobacco, but a guy from the shipwreck lot chucked over a half-empty pack of cigarettes. Bill lit one, sat down and shut his eyes.

It hit us quite suddenly.

Even with all the choppiness, there was no mistaking the no-go zone; it was like going from the merry-go-round onto the roller-coaster. As the boat lurched, we clung to the railing and took a face-full of seawater.

'Argh! That came out of nowhere!' cried Sean, as he clung for dear life onto the helm. Steadying himself, he quickly turned the boat around; we chugged desperately for a few moments, not seeming to get anywhere...then at last things calmed down. The boats collected on the edge of the zone, and waited.

I looked over at Bill; amazingly, he didn't seem to have stirred, and his eyes were still shut.

'Is he *asleep*?' called Sam, over the roar of the sea and the wind.

'No...look, his lips are moving,' I yelled back, then went *urrgh*, as we plunged back the other way.

Bill was passing his milpreve back and forth from one hand to the other, muttering louder now, eyes still closed. Every now and then he clutched the Saint Andrew pendant around his neck, still muttering.

I found myself shutting my eyes too, and 'praying'

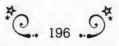

with him – if praying is what you'd call it. It was more a case of visualising Captain Quaid going to sleep, along with his army of horror-movie phantoms. Every now and then I half-opened my eyes to look at the horizon, just so I wouldn't throw up from the movement of the boat.

I have no idea how long I stayed there like that; maybe five minutes, maybe half an hour. But at some point I heard Bill say, 'It is done,' and I came back into the world and gazed out at the zone; amazingly, he was right. The torrential circle had unwound itself, and the waves just danced up and down same as everywhere else. What the hell the newspaper guys were making of all this, I hadn't a clue.

After that, we waited.

Sam and I didn't dive; we weren't allowed. Ty had explained that he'd be too busy filming to keep an eye on us.

To be honest I was relieved; didn't really fancy reliving the horrors I'd experienced down on that reef. On the other hand, what a big moment this would be! Recovering the remains of a nearly-three-hundred-year-old wreck, complete with valuable treasure: what a thing to witness! *If* they pulled it off, that is. Instead, Sam and I would have to content ourselves with the live stream from Ty's camera on the boat's monitor.

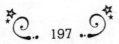

'OK,' said Sam, after the recovery team had set off. 'I'm going down below to watch. You coming?'

'I think I'll wait up here a bit, keep Bill company,' I said. 'Plus it's really rough; don't want to get seasick. At least up here I can watch the horizon.'

'OK,' said Sam. 'I'll yell up if anything good happens.' And he and Sean went down.

Nothing did happen for a while.

Then Bill began to get all agitated. 'What's up, Bill?' I asked.

'It's the divers,' he said. 'They've disturbed the spirits…ah yes, got me work cut out now.' He grunted and began rocking back and forth, chanting as he handled the stone and the saint, the saint and the stone, chanting, chanting…

Again, I shut my eyes and concentrated. I visualised the divers going down past drifting phantoms, undisturbed…down, down…scooping up armfuls of treasure while the ghost of Captain Quaid rested nearby, oblivious.

This was where I had trouble.

Quaid lying there, peaceful. Big, ugly Quaid, just slumbering away like a baby. My head went all wrong and mixed-up inside, and a different movie from the one I had the script for was nudging it out of the way. It was

a rerun of the one Beth had showed me in my dream: Quaid very much awake, and angry, and threatening…big, beefy face looming over me, as if I was Beth herself…

No, no…it was all wrong! Picture him *dead*, I told myself…I tried to fast-forward to the bit where his head had hit the table, and he was slumped on the floor, but here he was again, big and bulbous and looming…god, this was one powerful spirit; he was resisting me! Giving Bill a hard time too, by the sound of it: he was rocking and chanting, harder than ever.

We had to keep going. Maybe it wouldn't be easy for those guys down there, but maybe once they got hold of some of the stuff, then Quaid's power would wane…

'T's here!' said a voice beside me.

Oh no: Beth.

I opened my eyes. 'You? What are you doing here?'

'Ee'm a-hollerin' for me fit to bust, is why!' said Beth.

'No, I wasn't!' I protested. Oops: had Bill heard? I looked around: well, if he had heard anything, he wasn't letting on. Still rocking and chanting. I turned to Beth and repeated myself: 'You made a mistake. I wasn't calling you. I'm not ready for you yet.'

'Not ready! Ee were callin' and I'm *not* mistaken!'

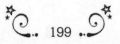

And with that, Beth pulled back her hand and smacked me in the face.

Yep: she *actually hit me*.

It was the first time I'd made contact with a ghost – and it wasn't what I'd expected, I can tell you. Well, not that I really had any idea what to expect. Just so you know, when a ghost thwacks you, it's a bit like being hit by a jellyfish. Yeah, the stinging kind. Only much…heavier, somehow. Heavy while at the same time passing right through you, if that makes any sense. Anyway, it *hurt*.

'Ow!' I cried, clutching my cheek. 'What d'you do that for?'

'Ee do make me 'mazed with all o' thy messin'!' yelled Beth. 'Come now, *don't* come now, thy Jed's *here*, no 'e *ain't*…augh!'

'Look, I wasn't calling you! I…I don't know, maybe you crept into my thoughts when I was trying to calm Quaid. But I didn't mean for that to happen! And…this is a really bad time, I–'

Thumple. Beth threw me another stinging swipe.

Sam emerged from the cabin. 'Kitty!' he cried. 'What the hell's going on?'

'I appear to be involved in a punch-up with a ghost,' I said.

'What? Not that Beth again?'

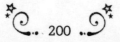

'Yep,' I said, rubbing my cheek.

Sam put his arms around me. 'Hey, leave her alone, OK?' he yelled in a non-specific direction. 'Come down below,' he told me. 'You're missing all the action. I've been calling you…they've got some of the jewels!'

'Better to stay up here, I reckon,' said Bill, making me jump. 'Look,' he added, pointing to the salvage vessel. 'They're comin' back up!'

Now Sean appeared on deck too; he revved up the engine and edged closer, so we could get a better look. He took us alongside the recovery boat and tethered us to it; now we were right at the centre of the action. A hefty chain was being winched up, and the divers were coming aboard; at the end of the chain was a cage. As soon as the cage appeared, laden with containers, a great cheer went up. You couldn't actually see what was in them, but it hardly mattered; by now, everyone knew that diamonds and pearls had been recovered, and excitement filled the air.

Another diver was mounting the stepladder beside the cage, carrying something bulky under one arm. He pulled out his breathing apparatus, pushed back his mask…and as he clung, dripping and breathless, to the stepladder, he held up the thing he was carrying. A big, black bell, dripping with seaweed.

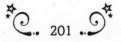

'It's from the *Venus*!' he cried. 'It says on here!' He wobbled as he held the bell up higher still – not that any of us was close enough to see the engraving. 'There's loads more jewels down there,' he cried hoarsely. 'And they're all from the *Venus*!'

'The *Venus*...' echoed Beth, staring.

Then I saw another figure lift out of the waves: bouffant blonde hair with Alice band, silk scarf around her neck, colourful sweater, arms back-to-front... I recognised the ghost of Harriet Jenkins, d. 1982. And although her head was still on the wrong way, her face was no longer filled with horror. She just drifted upwards, as if levitated by invisible balloons. And now here were the others, too: the 1950s guy; the one in the tweeds and the goggles, the Victorian lady...all floating up, bodies still mashed, but faces serene.

More cheering from all around. Cameras flashed from over on the newspaper boat. There was a carnival atmosphere, and the mood among these ghosts was the same – but only I could see them.

And what I had hoped and prayed would happen, seemed to be happening: they were freed! Stuck down there all this time, recruited by Quaid to keep people away from his hoard...and now the spell was broken! He'd lost his power over them.

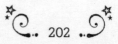

Where *was* Quaid, anyway? I wondered. But I didn't have to wonder for long.

'Quaid!' said Beth – and I saw she was looking at the rising cage.

Now it had completely cleared the waters, and hanging below it, desperately clinging on, was the familiar figure of Captain Zachary Quaid. Only now he seemed…smaller, if that was possible. Still fat; just sort of scaled-down, so that he could only have been about my height.

He was shouting, but the sound that was coming out of him was sort of metallic and shrill.

'No! Noooo!' he cried, and I could swear he was actually getting…no, was this possible?

It looked like he was actually *shrinking*. Yes: it *was* possible. As the cage rose higher and higher, so he shrank further, at the same time becoming broader and more squished. Soon his legs disappeared altogether, while his arms shortened and shortened until his hands, disproportionately large now, extended straight from his shoulders. Now his torso doubled over and his head shrivelled away into the brownish carapace that was forming itself out of his back. His fingers grew longer and bonier, and his thumbs fattened out into big pincers, until finally, Captain Quaid was a crab. Just a mute sea

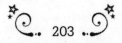

creature, clinging onto a stray piece of seaweed dangling from the cage.

As the cage came up to the level of the boat's deck, one of the divers leaned over, pulled the piece of seaweed free, and slung the Quaid-crab back into the sea.

'Wow!' I gasped.

'Brilliant, isn't it?' said Sam.

'More than you know,' I said.

'Ha! Good riddance!' said Beth.

'Oh Beth, you know what this means?' I said. 'You're free now! You can go over to the other side, and join your Jed… Oh, look! That's what they're doing!' I added, as I caught sight of the other ghosts. They had formed a circle and, with their poor distorted limbs extended awkwardly towards each other, they linked up and rose higher.

'Aye, I can feel they a-pullin' me to them,' said Beth.

'Are they? Well, there you go, then: this is your moment. This is where I would have called you back anyway…go!'

Beth rose up from the deck and began to drift towards them – then suddenly she gripped the rail and hung on, hovering horizontally. 'But how does ee *know* this'll bring me to Jed?'

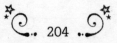

'Because…because he's not here, Beth! He's nowhere here in the mortal realm, I promise you. It's the only other place he could possibly be. Go on, Beth – just let go!'

She gazed up at the sky. 'My Jed…on the other side…'

'Yes!'

The circle rose higher still.

Beth let go with one hand and turned to look at them, hovering there in tweeds and big skirts and frazzled rags. 'My Jed…'

'Go on!'

Then at last she released her other hand, and away she flew. 'Goodbyyye…!' she called. She turned a couple of somersaults as she went, then reached out to the others with open arms. Harriet Jenkins let go of Norman Cavendish's hand, and invited her into the circle.

At this point it went all blurry; I could barely see through my tears. I waved. 'Go on, Beth…goodbye!'

'You all right?' asked Sam.

I gave a loud sniff. 'Oh yeah…it's just, Beth's gone now – for good.'

Sam slapped me on the back. 'Oh wow, that's brilliant! Good riddance; the nutter.'

I laughed through my tears.' 'Yeah…the nutter. Oh,

good luck, Beth!' I was sobbing now. 'I know you'll find him…I just know you will!'

Up and up went the circle, fading…soon, they were gone completely, leaving just the whistle of the wind and the roar of the sea.

# Reward

Last night I had a dream. I was Beth again, and I was walking through the deserted lanes of Pelporth. It was misty and kind of grey…I had the sense that it was just before dawn. Something big was about to happen, but I wasn't sure what it was. I just knew that I had to get down to the harbour.

When I got there, all I could see was this great mass of swirling mist. But I kept going. Beyond it, there was something…someONE I was meant to get to. I carried blindly on. Then, when the dark figure appeared before me; my heart went into a gallop. Yes! THIS was the reason I'd come here. I knew now…

'Jed!' I yelled, waking up – and scaring the wits out of

poor Flossie. 'Sorry,' I said, and explained about the dream. It was HIM, I told her: it was Jed! And I was happy now: I'd got them back together!

Flossie wasn't impressed. 'All you did was go down to the harbour before dawn, same as in that other dream when you were running away to sea,' she said. She couldn't see how I could tell it was anything more than just a repeat.

No, I explained: this was different. This was not just some memory. This was happening NOW. I can't really say how I knew it; I just did! And it wouldn't have happened without the destruction of Captain Quaid – I am sure of that. It was just as I thought: HE was keeping her here, out of spite and revenge. And I freed her.

I DID THAT – ME!! I brought Beth and Jed back together at last.

Amazing! Am feeling pretty good all round right now. ☺

---

The next few days were tense, while we waited for the Receiver of Wreck to decide who was the rightful owner. I didn't know who the Receiver of Wreck was, but I pictured Uncle Sean having to present himself to some grand personage in a big fancy chair, possibly

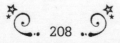

wearing a wig, who would eye him suspiciously, before dismissing him with a contemptuous wave.

Sean was on the phone *constantly*. Maro and Phoebe were a bundle of nerves. Even Winston the cockatoo seemed particularly bonkers. As for me, I half expected some horrible descendant of Captain Quaid, complete with bulbous nose and gouty leg, to turn up and claim everything.

After about a week, we moved on to Devon, and left them to it. Five days later, we were just mooching about in the Hippo, when Maro got a call. 'Aaaahh! *The-eh mou, thavmasio ta pethia!*' she yelled, and other similar OTT Greekisms, while she jiggled about and made the Hippo shake. The remains of the *Venus*, and its contents, were Sean's property. There was no one else.

The local news people went completely mental. It made the national news too.

So here we were, a few days later, back in Cornwall, at the Maritime Museum in Falmouth. There hadn't been time to clean things up – or even to salvage everything – but that wasn't the point. For now, people were just amazed at the discovery of this 285-year-old wreck, and wanted to come and have a gawp at the first finds. The timbers had all rotted away long ago, but there were cannon-shot, medals, coins, guns…all the

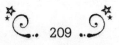

metal stuff, basically. So far just one cannon had been brought up – and of course there was the bell. It was still all covered in barnacles and stuff, but you could just make out the word *Venus* engraved on it.

Sean and Ty were being interviewed by some telly reporter with a head too big for his body.

'…So how was it that you came to discover the long-lost wreck?' asked the telly guy.

'Quite by accident!' said Sean. 'We don't search for wrecks; our job is to record marine life.'

'So you just…stumbled across it?' said Mr Bighead Telly Guy.

'Yes,' said Sean. 'It was pure luck, really – that's all.'

Sam, Floss and I all looked at each other, relieved that Sean had done as he'd promised and not given anything away.

'What went through your mind, when you first saw the diamonds?' the interviewer asked Ty.

'Well, at first we thought it must be a shoal of silvery fish – but I soon realised it wasn't that. The conditions didn't give us much time, but I managed to reach out and grab a handful…'

'…And the rest is history, as they say!' added Mr Bighead Telly Guy, beaming. Then he suddenly turned all Serious, and looked at the camera. 'But there's a dark

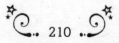

secret lurking in the history of this particular ship. A centuries-old legend tells of strange ghostly sightings of the *Venus* – and how those who'd experienced these visions all met with a sticky end.'

I felt my face flush. 'What's he doing talking about that?' I hissed to Sam.

'What do you think?' said Sam. 'Look at him – he's milking it.'

Bighead Telly Guy turned back to Sean. 'What do you make of these stories, Mr Goodstow? And what do you think might happen now the wreck of this ship has been recovered? Are you worried?'

I squirmed.

Sean laughed it off. 'Well, you know, I'm not sure I'd take those stories too seriously…'

Again Sam, Floss and I exchanged glances; we knew differently.

'…but if there *were* any truth to them,' Sean went on – and I swear he shot me a little glance at this point, before adding: 'I'd say that the cosmic order of things has been restored. All is well, now that the *Venus* has come home to rest at last!' He beamed out at the audience, raising his arm triumphantly. And then – yes! – he winked at me.

As a wave of applause went around the room,

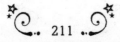

I thought, *Yup: everything's changed for good now.* Quaid's power was gone; the treasure had at last been brought home, and the ship's last captain and his wife had been reunited. The cosmic order, as Sean said, was restored, and neither I nor anyone else was going to get hypnotised into going over the edge of a cliff. Phew!

I was so busy thinking about this, the next thing I knew, there was an even bigger wave of applause. 'Hang on, what did he say?' I asked Flossie.

'He's just said how much they think the jewels will be worth, Kitty. Wake up! Yaaaaay!'

'So you're a millionaire!' said the telly guy.

Sean looked slightly embarrassed. 'Well, no, not me personally – the majority will go to our research fund. And then there are the people who helped, the ones without whom this could never have happened...'

*Bill.* I looked around for him; although he'd come in with us, he'd sort of skulked off, and was now hiding in the back, like he was pretending not to be there. I turned to Ashley and grabbed her hand. 'Come on,' I said, and together we pushed our way over to him. His eyes widened as he saw us, and he gave a little shake of the head, like he didn't want any attention drawn to him.

So we looked the other way, all nonchalant; then

Ashley, arms folded, edged closer and said, 'Congratulations, Bill!'

'Ah, no, congratulations to *you*,' said Bill.

'But you're getting a big reward, Bill,' said Ashley. 'Dad said so, remember?'

A moment later, having finished with the TV interview, Sean appeared beside us. 'Hello, Bill, I don't suppose you'd come up and say a word—'

'Not on your Nelly!' said Bill.

'All right, all right, I won't mention you by name, not if you don't want me to,' said Sean. 'But this has all been down to you; I hardly did anything. I feel like a complete fraud! We should split this, fifty-fifty.'

Bill waved his hand. 'Oh no, I don't need that much, you save it for your research.'

Sean laughed and patted him on the back. 'That's kind of you, Bill, but I won't be put off that easily! You think about it for a while, eh? Plenty of time.'

Bill put his hand on Sean's arm. 'All right, well, don't you forget young Kitty here. She played an important part too, y'know.'

'Of course,' said Sean, smiling at me. 'Maro will put it by for you, Kitty.'

'Oh, yeah…uh-huh,' was about all I could manage to say. Can't say I wasn't a bit disappointed not to have

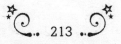

the cash myself. Being a kid sucks sometimes.

After that, Ashley and I wandered around a bit, looking at the stuff on show.

'Hey, Ashley!' came a voice from behind us. We looked up; it was old lover-boy, Oliver. 'Hey, congratulations!' he said. 'This is just…so cool!'

'Uh…yeah,' said Ashley, not really looking directly at him.

'Yeah…' said Oliver, nodding. 'Your dad's, like… really clever.'

'Oh well, you know…it was kind of a team effort,' said Ashley. I couldn't help noticing how un-gushy she was.

'So anyway…' said Oliver. He cleared his throat, ruffled his hair. 'You wanna go to a movie sometime?'

'Oh…thanks,' said Ashley, 'but I don't really bother with the movies. Oh, Kitty, look who's over there! Good to see you, Oliver…bye!'

'Yeah, cool, whatever,' said Oliver.

Ashley took me by the arm, and whizzed me away. 'Ooh, that was not easy,' she said.

'I figured,' I said. 'But well done.'

'Yeah, well…funny how he changed his tune as soon as he thought my dad had come into some cash. Never gave me a second glance before.'

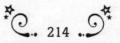

'I'm glad you realised that,' I said. 'I had kind of noticed, but I didn't know how to tell you.'

'Hmm...' said Ashley. 'Guess I was kind of deluded – lookin' for *lurv* in the wrong place! Bit like your ghost, Beth Trewin.'

This made me squeal with laughter – especially the way she said the word 'lurv'. It was good to see her not taking herself too seriously. Then I noticed something in a display case; an ivory comb. 'Oh my god, look; that comb...it was Beth's!'

Ashley peered. 'Really?'

'Yeah! I saw it in one of the dreams. She used it to hold her hair in place under her headscarf – when she was pretending to be a boy.'

'Oh, wow.'

I sighed as I stared at the blackened comb, with its broken teeth and its curved, worn spine. Coming face-to-face with something that had belonged to the living, breathing Beth was suddenly all a bit much; I felt my throat close up as I reached out and touched the glass cabinet. 'Oh, Ashley...I miss her!'

'*Really?* said Ashley.

'Um...' I sniffed back the tears. 'Yeah, I know... weird, huh?'

'No, not weird,' said Ashley. 'Totally understandable.'

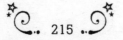

'It's funny how somebody can be a total pain in the bum, and yet…on some level, you kind of…*like* them? Does that make any sense?'

'Oh, *totally*,' said Ashley.

'Do you feel the same way about Megan, then?' I asked.

'I guess I do, sort of. Though I never realised it till just now. I remember how things were, before the teasing started…and way before she went off the rails. She plaited my hair and showed me how to skip: she was totally the skipping champion back in year five, I remember. Whereas I was rubbish. I hope she'll have a better life now.'

I sighed. 'At least she's still around to have a shot at that. But Beth…I'll never see her again; ever.'

'I know,' said Ashley. 'But you did a good thing for her. An amazing thing!'

'Yeah…I guess.'

That evening, I made my excuses after dinner and wandered out to the Logan Stone, alone. I needed some time by myself, just to think about stuff.

As I perched on the lichen-covered rocks beside it, I thought back to the day we'd first arrived, when Sam, Flossie and I had come out here with Ashley. God, that

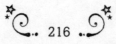

seemed so long ago now! Like, a *lifetime* ago.
I remembered Ashley talking about spriggans; the spirits
of the giants that supposedly lurked in places like this.
They swelled up to giant size, she'd said, and they…ha!
They guarded treasure. How like Captain Quaid,
I thought now. Quaid, who'd seemed so gigantic, so
powerful – who *was* powerful, and literally larger than
life…ending up shrunk down to crab-size. Crabby little
nobody.

Then there were those other crabby little nobodies
with their fake treasures, Howie and Aidan Kernon.
They'd also probably seemed so big and powerful to
Megan, until their nasty little racket was exposed. They
might not literally have shrivelled away into little
harmless crabs like Captain Quaid…but they might just
as well have done.

I did miss Beth. But I'd get over it. Occupational
hazard, I suppose. I decided to head back to the Hippo.
I reached up, put my hand on the Logan Stone and
pushed: it didn't move an inch.

Still wicked. Which was good to know.

# Glossary of Maro-isms

*Fantastika!* [fan-**tas**-ti-ka]......fantastic!

*Pethaki-mou* [pe-**tha**-ki moo]......my children

*Kitaki-mou* [Kit-**ak**-i moo]......my little Kitty

*Kitta na thiss!* [**kee**-ta na theess]......look at this!

*Kali epitychia* [ka-**lee** ep-i-ti-**hyah**]......good luck

*The-eh mou!* [theh-**eh** moo]......my god!

*Thavmasio* [thav-**mas**-i-o]......wonderful

*Ta pethia* [ta peth-**ya**]......children/kids

# Acknowledgements

My thanks to friends Keren David and Sara Fonseca-Williams for reading this story when it was still a bit muddled, and giving me excellent advice! Thanks also Sarah Riddle of the Falmouth Museum, archaeologist Dave Parham and shipping historian Richard Larn for their professional input. And as ever, thanks to my cousin Mat for his help with the police-related info.

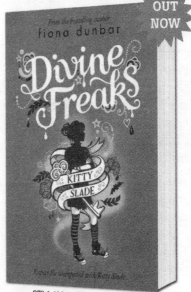

No rainbows.
No pink.
No sparkles.
No ordinary fairytale.

978 1 408 30312 2 PB £5.99
978 1 408 31234 6 eBook

978 1 408 30737 3 PB £5.99
978 1 408 31264 3 eBook

978 1 408 31262 9 PB £5.99
978 1 408 31370 1 eBook

ORCHARD BOOKS
Celebrating 25 Years
www.orchardbooks.co.uk

R J ANDERSON

www.orchardbooks.co.uk

Don't miss the stunning new series from Holly Webb,
bestselling author of *Rose*

## Magic will always find a way...

In a world where magic is
outlawed, Lily runs wild and
neglected. Once rich and
powerful magicians, now
Lily's family hide away in their
crumbling house, while her
older sister, Georgie, is trained
secretly in magic.

But when Lily discovers her
parents' dark plan to use
Georgie in a terrible plot to
restore the country to its
magical glory, she knows
she must rescue her sister –
and flee...

978 1 40831 349 7 £5.99 PB

ORCHARD BOOKS
Celebrating 25 Years
www.orchardbooks.co.uk

**www.orchardbooks.co.uk**